A CANDLELIGHT ROMANCE

CANDLELIGHT ROMANCES

SUMMER MAGIC

Frances Carfi Matranga

A CANDLELIGHT ROMANCE

Dedicated to my daughter Francine

Published by
Dell Publishing Co., Inc.
1 Dag Hammarskjold Plaza
New York, New York 10017

Dell ® TM 681510, Dell Publishing Co., Inc.

ISBN: 0-440-17962-9

Printed in the United States of America
First printing—May 1979

Chapter One

She was actually on her way to the Caribbean! It didn't seem possible, thought Kathy, pressing her pert nose to the window of the jetliner as they passed puffy clouds that resembled buttered popcorn with the sunshine spilling over them. Flying was a new and thrilling experience for her, and she pinched herself to make sure she really was on the plane and not dreaming at home in her own bed.

To think it was only little more than a week since she received the exciting phone call that was to change the course of her life! She smiled as she remembered how nonchalantly she had taken the receiver from her mother's hand to say hello to Lucy Clark. Mrs. Clark was a widowed friend of her mother's, and she came to the point at once. Kathy could still recall almost every word of their conversation.

"Kathy, my dear, how would you like to work in Haiti for the summer, all expenses paid?"

It was so unexpected, it left her speechless.

"You're between jobs, aren't you?" Mrs. Clark's pleasantly modulated voice came over the wire smoothly. "Ada told me a couple of days ago that you quit your job with the insurance office."

"Uh . . . that's right." What else had her mother told Mrs. Clark? The next remark provided the answer.

"That boss of yours should have known better than to get fresh with a nice decent girl like you. Listen, dear, I just now explained the situation to Ada. She doesn't like the idea of your going off to another country by yourself, but it's your decision to make. You're twenty-one, after all, even though to your mother you'll always be the baby of the family—you know, dear, she's been clinging to you a little too much since your father died. It might do you both good to be apart for a while."

Kathy understood. Her three older siblings were married and had moved away from home. But she still lived with her mother who, naturally, was inclined to be possessive toward her and to worry over her unnecessarily. It hadn't developed into a real problem yet, but Kathy was aware that it might. Since her father's death some months before, a slow and subtle change had come about, with her mother invading her privacy more and more, wanting to share every area of her life, even her thoughts. Apparently her friend Lucy had noticed, and Kathy recognized the wisdom in Lucy's advice.

"Yes, I understand," she said briefly, for her mother was sitting nearby listening to the one-sided conversation. "Did you say Haiti?" It seemed like the other end of the world to Kathy, perhaps not in miles but certainly in culture. "What kind of job is it?" she asked cautiously, though already she could feel a twinge of excitement stirring in the pit of her stomach.

"Secretary to my brother, more or less," said Mrs. Clark. "He's doing research there and soaking up atmosphere for a novel based on that country, and he needs someone to take dictation and type up the manuscript. His typing is atrocious. He tried a local woman and it didn't work out, so last night he phoned and offered *me* the job. But I'm getting set to spend a month in Canada with a friend. I thought of you and told him I'd see what I could do. What do you say, Kathy? If it's yes, Scott will wire the plane fare and you can leave just as quickly as possible, no need for a passport or shots. A job like this doesn't come along every day, and he's offering a fabulous salary. By the way, his housekeeper and Tony are with him, so it's all very proper. Tony's his son, who's twelve. Scott lost his wife in a car accident almost a year ago, and he's been raising the boy with Mrs. Maguire's help. Do you want the position?"

Kathy had to sit down, feeling suddenly breathless. This was Scott Blackburn they were talking about—a famous author!

"I-I—" she began.

Mrs. Clark cut in persuasively, "I should think it'd be the kind of work you'd enjoy, what with your love for books and the fact that you do some writing for children. Oh, congratulations, my dear. I hear you recently sold your first story. Listen, Kathy, you don't need a college education to assist Scott, just proficiency in spelling and punctuation. And since you already know how to set up a manuscript . . . As for salary . . ." She named a figure that sounded too good to be true. With living expenses and transportation paid as well, how can I refuse? thought Kathy. Why, it would enable her to furnish one side of her bedroom as a work study. Desk, filing cabinet, electric typewriter— everything the neophyte writer could want. Her old manual portable skipped when she typed fast, and the card table she worked on was getting wobbly. This was a wonderful opportunity not only for the money, but to broaden her horizons. She'd always wanted to travel.

But Haiti? Land of blacks, voodoo, and poverty? A pucker appeared between her eyebrows, and ominous question marks formed in her mind as she recalled some of the weird things she'd heard about that country that was like no other in the world. Witch doctors. Black magic. People possessed by pagan gods. Zombies.

Did she really want to go to so foreign a place—a stranger in a mysterious land? Why, she'd be utterly on her own should something go wrong.

Nothing's going to go wrong, chided the eager adventuresome side of her nature. You're healthy, capable, intelligent, and you've solved problems before.

7

And you wouldn't be alone; you'd have Mr. Blackburn to turn to.

Listen, who can say what might happen? warned the little voice of caution inside her. You could catch a dread disease.

Now she was being ridiculous, Kathy admonished herself. If the author considered Haiti safe enough for his young son, then surely it was safe for her. After all, it wasn't a total wilderness inhabited by savages. And there were hospitals there. As for those tales she had heard, most were probably legends and superstitions. She'd be a fool to turn down this once-in-a-lifetime chance to work with a world-famous author, especially since she had similar aspirations in the field of children's literature. Think what being exposed to Mr. Blackburn's talent could do for her, she told herself; think what she could learn from him in the way of technique, even work habits. Her own were far from organized.

Kathy knew that the author was of English ancestry, born and raised in the United States, and that he made his home in California. His very first book, *Roar of the Dragon*, had catapulted him to fame. A political novel of China, it had made the best-seller list, and was followed by *Too Late, My Love*—a tragic French historical romance that was translated into a dozen languages and made into a successful movie. Kathy had read both books and thought them exceptionally well done. She had wept copious tears over the French romance when the hero's sweetheart died to save his life.

From his books, she would judge Scott Blackburn to be a thoughtful and sensitive person. And now he was working on his third novel—another potential best seller, no doubt—and to think the opportunity to assist him had come to *her*, ordinary little Kathy Miller!

"Kathy? You there?" Mrs. Clark's voice over the wire snapped Kathy out of her reverie, which had swooshed through her mind in a matter of seconds. "Would you like a little time to think it over?"

8

"I already have. Tell him yes," said Kathy. She laid the phone in its cradle and turned to face her mother, who was chewing nervously on her lower lip. "Well," she said, "I've committed myself."

"You're really going to take the job? Oh, dear! You ought to take time to think it over. If it were England or France or someplace like that . . . But Haiti!"

Kathy sat on the sofa with her mother, a determined look on her pretty face. "I've already thought about it. That's where the job is, and I want it, Mother."

"But you've never been away from home before."

"Then it's about time." Kathy spoke firmly. "This offer is a godsend, just when I need a job and am free to accept it. Can you imagine, I'll be working for a celebrated author! I'll be involved in the sort of work I myself am interested in. How many girls have such an opportunity to visit a foreign land and earn good money at the same time? Oh, I can't believe it!" She jumped to her feet, too excited to remain still. "Haiti, here I come!" she cried, flinging out her arms and doing a pirouette.

Her mother rose also. Both of medium height, they resembled each other. Ada Miller was still attractive, though her blond hair was turning gray and the contour of her face had lost its firmness. There were lines around her eyes and mouth that seemed to deepen as she fretted. "What about the voodoo business? There are witch doctors there, like in Africa."

"Oh, Mom, please don't try to discourage me. And be sensible. What have I to do with witch doctors? I'll be living with an American family."

"But I've heard—"

"Mother, please!" Taking her mother by the hand, Kathy drew her down with her on the sofa. "Try not to get upset. I'm going, and that's all there is to it. And I wish you wouldn't look as if you were going to burst into tears."

Her mother managed a tremulous smile. "I'll be lonely with you gone all summer, honey. With your brothers living out of town and your sister busy with her own family, I don't get to see them all that often."

"There are ways to combat loneliness," Kathy said firmly. "There's volunteer work, and you could go out more with your friends instead of sticking so close to this little apartment. Dad left you enough money from the sale of our house so you don't have to scrimp. Stop living for your children and start living for yourself—please? You won't have me to cook for all summer, so eat out once in a while, huh?" She chucked her under the chin playfully. "Live it up for a change. And stop worrying about me. I'm a big girl now, or hadn't you noticed?"

Mrs. Miller gave a sigh of acquiescence. "Well . . . at least I'm glad it's Lucy's brother you'll be working for. No doubt he's a gentleman and wouldn't *think* of pinching your bottom, like that son of a gun in the insurance office." Kathy burst out laughing at that, and her mother ended up giggling too.

They hugged each other, and Kathy said, "I've a million things to do before I leave. There's my Sunday school class; I'll have to see about a substitute teacher to take over for me. And I've got to let my friends know, and I'll need to borrow an extra suitcase and—oh, dear!—I have to buy a bathing suit, my old one is shot." She got up. "I'd better start going through my wardrobe right now. There's sewing to do. Oh, I mustn't forget to take my alarm clock and my hair dryer and—" She broke off with a laugh and took a deep breath. "First thing, I'd better just calm down. But, oh, it's all so quick and unexpected."

"Then it's all set? You're going for sure?"

"For sure, Mom."

And here she was on her way. Despite her elation, nervousness set in as the jetliner neared Haiti. From what she'd gathered from a second conversation with Mrs. Clark, Scott was renting a furnished summer home in the mountains somewhere above the city of

Port-au-Prince, where there was no telephone. He had called his sister from a public phone and had returned to it the next day at a pre-set time to receive her answer confirming Kathy's acceptance of the job offer.

Suppose I find him hard to work for? Kathy found herself thinking. Suppose I can't stand the tropical heat? She was committed for June, July, and August. Suppose—

She put a brake on the negative thoughts. She had given her word that upon accepting the position she would see it through, and her word was her bond, a fact she took pride in.

What was he like, she mused, leaning back against the headrest and closing her eyes. That he was thirty-five and a widower, she knew. With a son of twelve, obviously he had married young. Was he really as attractive as the photo on his book jackets? Not handsome, exactly, but so distinguished-looking with that finely chiseled head, strong proud nose, and those slight hollows beneath his cheekbones. Dark wavy hair. His eyes—blue? Difficult to tell from a black and white picture. They could just as well be green, gray, or hazel. Set beneath thick black brows, they held a faraway expression, as though he lived in a world all his own. Well, in a way, didn't every fiction writer create his own world, even many worlds?

Scott Blackburn—her lips formed his name. A good name, a strong-sounding name, she thought, and it fit his face well. Despite that ivory tower expression, she felt he was the sort of person who could be relied upon in a crisis.

"Pardon?"

Kathy's eyes flew open, and she realized she had spoken aloud. The man sitting next to her had boarded the plane in Miami, but she'd been so preoccupied with her thoughts, she hardly had noticed.

"I was thinking aloud, I'm afraid," she confessed with an embarrassed laugh.

He appeared to be in his late thirties or early forties

11

and sported a small dark mustache that suited him well. Slim and elegant, he had even features and soft dark eyes that could melt a woman's heart, Kathy thought. Almost too handsome, she decided. Anyone who looked like that must have females falling all over him and was bound to be self-centered. A quick glance revealed that the trousers of his tan lightweight suit were sharply creased, his brown shoes highly polished. He wore a red carnation in his lapel, and she liked the smell of his cologne. She could see an expensive ring on his right hand—a ruby, surely?—and a matching stickpin in his tie. The man looked as though he had just stepped out of a bandbox.

She saw his eyes appraising her long blond hair as he said, "You mentioned Scott Blackburn? The writer?"

"Why, yes." And as he waited expectantly, she explained she was going to spend the summer as a secretary for the author who was working on his Haitian novel.

"Is that so?" He appeared interested. "Permit me to introduce myself, Pierre Rollet. I live in Haiti, although my business takes me to Miami quite often. I own a gift shop in Port-au-Prince, and I export native handicrafts." He spoke precise English without contractions and with a delightful French accent.

"How do you do, Mr. Rollet. I'm Kathy Miller from Irvington, New York. Do you know Mr. Blackburn by any chance?"

"I do. And you?"

She shook her head. "I got the job through his sister. She's a friend of my mother's. Have you read his books?"

"Being French, I got hold of a paperback of his historical novel set in nineteenth-century France. The man has a way with words, I must admit. Is this your first trip to Haiti, mademoiselle?" And as Kathy nodded, he added, "You will find it interesting, I am sure. One thing about Haiti, it is nothing if not interesting. Or should I say—different?"

"You can say *that* again. From the little I know . . ." Kathy's voice trailed off.

He smiled. "You are referring to the *vodoun* or *vaudou*?"

"You mean voodoo? Well, yes. Tell me something, will you, Mr. Rollet? I understand the country is predominantly Roman Catholic. So how come the people still practice the old African voodoo religion?"

"There is a saying in Haiti that ninety percent of the people are Catholic and one hundred percent *vaudou*. The latter, you see, is the traditional popular belief, and Catholicism, also accepted, has been superimposed upon it. The two religions are practiced concurrently and even interchangeably."

Seeing the perplexed expression on Kathy's face, this new acquaintance went on to explain more fully, "In other words, there is much borrowing from Catholicism to use as trappings for *vaudou*. For example, you know those little pictures of the saints? In *vaudou*, Papa Legba is the heavenly gatekeeper, and pictures of Saint Peter are used to represent him. Damballah Ouedo, the snake god, is represented by Saint Patrick; and pictures of the Madonna are used to represent the feminine god, Ezili-Freda, the goddess of love and fertility. She is loving and kind, but also erotic. Men pray to her, dance to her, fall in love with her. There are many many gods, and Catholicism will never succeed in abolishing them, I fear."

"Oh, I do wish I'd had time to study up before coming," she fretted. "But it was all so sudden, this job offer, and there were so many odds and ends to tuck in before leaving. But thanks for filling me in. And since you're so well informed, what about zombies? That's *weird*."

The Frenchman laughed at the face she made. *"Oui.* Many things in Haiti are weird, as you put it."

13

"But the zombie bit is so farfetched. It's *got* to be just a legend."

"You think so?" An enigmatic smile hovered about Pierre Rollet's lips. "My dear young lady, I have resided in Haiti a dozen years or more. You will admit one can learn a great deal about a country in that length of time? Very well, I will tell you something that is written in Haitian law. The Criminal Code specifies that anyone practicing witchcraft on men to turn them into zombies shall be guilty of murder even if the victims do not die."

There was a dramatic pause during which Kathy's deep brown eyes widened.

"Does that sound as though it refers to a legend?"

She shrugged helplessly. "It's too fantastic. Really, now, when a body is dead, it's dead. How can one be dead and still move about? I think you're putting me on."

Pierre Rollet chuckled and patted her arm with a manicured hand. "But you are intrigued, *oui*?" Quickly sobering, he said, "Truly, mademoiselle, I am serious. The Haitian Criminal Code really does state that. And why? Because there have been many documented— hear this, *documented*—cases of zombies from all over the land. I myself know a man who paints pictures for me to sell who experienced this kind of thing. A few years ago his eldest son suddenly took ill and died. The father witnessed the funeral and the burial, which took place within a day or so because of the tropical climate, you understand. Yet only last year in a distant town he recognized his son working in a field of sugarcane. The young man did not know his father, nor could he speak. He had become, literally, a robot. By the time the distraught father was able to contact the police, the boy had disappeared."

At Kathy's incredulous look, Pierre went on, "No one knows for sure, but one theory is that someone had given him a secret drug which caused suspended

14

animation, and then revived him later with an antidote. Of course, his mind was virtually destroyed."

Kathy was appalled. Could such a thing be? Mr. Rollet obviously was an intelligent man, and he seemed to believe it.

"But why?" she asked. "Why would anyone do such a thing?"

The Frenchman raised expressive brows and shrugged. "Who can say for sure? Sometimes the motive is revenge. Sometimes greed. Zombies can be sold to distant planters for a good price. They obey orders and work steadily and tirelessly without recompense."

Kathy fell silent as she digested all this, hardly knowing what to believe. It brought an old proverb to mind: that truth was stranger than fiction. But *that* strange? She shivered.

Pierre gave her a teasing smile. "Do not worry, my dear, chances are you will not run into one. Is Monsieur Blackburn meeting you at the airport?"

She nodded, fingering her necklace. "He'll be looking for a blonde in a white dress, with red beads and earrings. I don't think I'll be hard to spot, do you?"

"Who could miss such a pretty young lady?" said Pierre gallantly. "You look as American as your name."

"*Merci*, monsieur. I know a little French. Look, I really appreciate our discussion. I'm eager to learn all I can about Haiti. Of course, typing Mr. Blackburn's manuscript will be an education in itself, what with all the research he's done. I'm really looking forward to it."

"Perhaps we will meet again during your stay," he suggested. "The author is renting the Devereaux estate in the mountains while the family is in France. It is a long drive, but should you come into the capital I hope you will visit my shop." He took out his wallet and handed her his card. "Should you ever find yourself in difficulty in the city, please do not hesitate to call me. My telephone number is on the card."

15

"Why, thank you, monsieur. It's good to know I already have a friend in Haiti." She surely would look up his shop one day during her free time and buy some gifts to send home.

The pilot came on the loudspeaker to announce they were approaching their destination.

Looking out the window, Kathy could see the blue waters of the bayfront of Port-au-Prince. There was a luxury liner in the harbor and numerous small boats. Peddler crafts loaded with fruit and other wares were paddling toward the ship. The city itself was hemmed in on three sides by rugged mountains. She could see white beaches, swaying palm trees, and white, tile-roofed houses. Her stomach churned with excitement. They were almost there.

"You know," said Pierre suddenly, "he is a brilliant man, Blackburn, but temperamental. He has changed since the tragic death of his wife, according to his housekeeper. It must have been a terrible shock to him, of course." He hesitated. "I am afraid you have your work cut out for you, my dear. Still, who knows—perhaps the presence of a young lady like yourself will have a steadying effect upon him."

She wanted to ask what he meant, but the FASTEN YOUR SEATBELTS sign flashed on just then, and in the excitement of watching the plane touch down, she forgot.

Her new friend saw her through customs, and they went into the waiting room together.

I'm in *Haiti*, thought Kathy, a tiny tremor feathering along her spine. I'm here!

Chapter Two

There weren't too many people in the waiting room, and Kathy recognized her new boss at once. As the light eyes set in a sun-bronzed face leveled upon her, she felt her heart quiver within her breast, and a strange, swift turmoil of emotion erupted, like firecrackers going off inside her, leaving her shaken. She tried to pull herself together as he walked toward her. Never had the sight of any man affected her this way.

He was tall and wore a light-gray knitted sport shirt and charcoal slacks. Though slim, his body looked strong as steel, muscular, as though he exercised regularly. His eyes were gray, with the merest hint of blue, like wood smoke. Not handsome in any conventional sense, he nevertheless was extremely attractive and masculine.

But why, Kathy wondered uneasily, did he seem so surprised at the sight of her?

"You're Miss Miller?" Did she imagine it or was there disapproval in the baritone voice?

"That's right," she said with a tentative smile. "And you're Mr. Blackburn." There was no answering smile, and an uncomfortable pause followed.

"Well, then, let's get going," he said brusquely. "Oh, hello, Rollet."

"*Bonjour*, monsieur."

"We met on the plane," explained Kathy, "and Mr. Rollet was kind enough to see me through customs. I have my tourist card, so I guess I'm all set. Good-bye,

Mr. Rollet. I hope to visit your shop one of these days. Do you mail gifts direct from the store?"

"Indeed. And I shall look forward to seeing you again, mademoiselle." He bowed over her hand in the continental manner, and then she followed her escort out into the sultry afternoon heat to where a battered Jeep stood parked. The author placed her suitcases in back and helped her into the front passenger seat, and then went around to the other side and got in behind the wheel. Kathy rummaged in her handbag for her sunglasses and slipped them on, wondering why he hadn't offered the Frenchman a lift, since they knew each other. Really, he wasn't very polite, nor had he made her feel welcome.

She studied his profile as he drove and couldn't help but admit it was striking, strong, and manly—carved with precision.

"Do I meet with your approval?" he asked suddenly, and she flushed and turned her face away.

She didn't reply to the sardonic question and neither of them spoke again until some fifteen minutes later when they approached a village in the hills overlooking the capital. To break the awkward silence, Kathy asked where they were.

"That's Pétionville ahead, named after the first president," he told her. "It's a residential suburb of the Port-au-Prince elite, and also a hangout for wealthy tourists."

"Elite?" she questioned, wanting to know more.

"The light-skinned Haitians. Mulattoes and such. The aristocrats."

He shifted to a lower gear as they approached a rough section in the steep road ascending the sloping sides of the mountain. Along the way, atop the red clay banks on either side of the road, were humble peasant huts, picturesque with their palm or banana-frond roofs. Kathy saw an occasional goat browsing here and there, and natives coming and going along the sides of the road, some on foot, some riding donkeys. Most of

18

the women wore colorful bandannas. Kathy was all eyes and gasped with pleasure at the sight of large trees laden with gorgeous flame-colored blossoms.

"How beautiful! What are they called, those trees?"

"Flamboyants," he replied briefly. She wondered if he was always so laconic.

Soon they were driving through the center of Pétionville past a square lined with cypress trees. Kathy saw a church, and a building bearing a sign that said HABANEX, which her companion, in answer to her question, explained was a banana company. She had the feeling that unless she asked questions he would not speak to her at all, and it irked her to be so ignored. After all, she had come more than two thousand miles to work with him, and the least he could do was show a little warmth.

On they went, twisting up the side of the mountain, with the air growing noticeably cooler, though the sun was still a sizzling yolk in the bright blue sky. Kathy's long straight hair was whipping about in the breeze, and she reached into her handbag for a barrette to clip it back from her face.

They passed cornfields and, occasionally, glimpsed huts through the foliage flanking the unpaved road. A pretty brown girl, accompanied by a tiny boy who was chewing on a piece of sugarcane almost as long as he was tall, waved to them as the Jeep went by. Kathy returned the greeting, noting with some surprise that the little fellow was naked. Live and learn, she thought with wry humor, as the road continued to wind up the mountain past Kenscoff, where villas, vintage Victorian mansions and humble huts contrasted vividly with one another.

A little later, the Jeep pulled up at a single gasoline pump in front of a small store.

"Where are we now?" she asked.

"Furcy. We get a few of our supplies here. For the rest we go down to the city."

They got out of the vehicle and stretched their legs

while a boy filled the tank. Looking about, Kathy saw a building with a marquee announcing an old American movie.

She stepped back as a pig crossed the road in front of her and began rooting among the shrubbery on the other side. Several chickens wandered about aimlessly; and across the way, in the shade of a wooden building with a tin roof, stood a white goat nibbling on nearby foliage.

Soon they were bumpily off again. It was more a trail than a road after Furcy, and the vegetation on either side became denser as they continued winding their way ever upward. To Kathy it seemed they must be ascending one of the tallest mountains in all Haiti. Then the road leveled off and as they rounded a curve, a breathtaking view opened up before them.

"Oh, please," she cried, "would you stop the Jeep a minute and let me look?"

He obliged, and she sat in awe viewing a whole panorama of mountain ranges and deep valleys, lush jungles, and a gridded geometry of sugarcane dotted with barely distinguishable clusters of huts. Several thin plumes of smoke drifted up from outdoor cooking fires. A blanket of clouds lay off in the distance below eye level, with mountain peaks pushing through so that the clouds collared them. Directly below Kathy, the mountainside sloped down and away like a vast carpet, accented with the scarlet of flamboyant trees and other blossoms. To the west unfolded the city of Port-au-Prince with its deep blue harbor; and, beyond, Gonave Island in the bay, misty and mysterious. Never had Kathy seen so beautiful, so stupendous, so breathtaking a view.

"It's gorgeous!"

"Look there." Scott Blackburn pointed to doll figures hoeing in a distant field. "That's a *coumbite*—a work group," he said, volunteering information for the first time. "Men get together and take turns working in one another's fields. They do that all over Haiti and sing while they work. Afterward they have a party."

Kathy's head kept swiveling as she enjoyed the visual feast, not wanting to miss anything.

He started the Jeep and turned off onto another dirt road and shifted gears. Dense foliage closed in on them again, making a narrow green tunnel of the road. Soon they turned off into a level clearing, circled a drive and rolled to a stop in front of a large, old two-story house.

The first floor was fronted by a covered porch, the second floor by a balcony. Both were trimmed with wrought-iron railings. The paint on the house had weathered to a soft bluish-gray that was not unpleasant. The shutters and other trim seemed freshly painted and gleamed white. There was an expanse of lawn in front and on one side, and a patio on the other side; and purple bougainvillea and red and yellow hibiscus shaded the porch. From the rear an oak tree towered over the house.

Scott sprang from the Jeep and extended a hand to Kathy. Then he collected her luggage. A stout gray-haired woman with a pleasant face and a bosom like a rolltop desk had appeared on the porch at their arrival and stood awaiting them. Kathy preceded him up the steps.

"Miss Miller—Mrs. Maguire."

"Hello. You must be the housekeeper," said Kathy.

The woman nodded and ran an appraising glance over her, then focused on her face with bright blue eyes. "Well, now, 'tis a pretty lass you are. Welcome, dearie. Just call me Molly."

"Thank you." Kathy smiled at her, grateful for her warmth. "And I'm Kathy."

"I was waiting impatiently to get a look at you," Molly admitted candidly, adding, "You'll do just fine, I'll wager." She had a motherly air about her that appealed to Kathy, and she obviously had decided to be her friend.

They stepped inside. The entry hall had a polished

21

mahogany floor and ran the length of the house, separating it into two wings. There were several doors leading off to rooms on either side, and Kathy could see into a large living room to her immediate right, and a dining room on the left.

As they approached the staircase at the rear of the hall, a young Haitian woman appeared in the kitchen doorway to their left. Molly introduced her to Kathy, while Scott continued on upstairs with the luggage.

"This be Claudine Buteau," said Molly. "She lives with her family in the cottage out back and helps me with the cooking."

"Hello, Claudine."

"*Bo-jou*, mam'selle." Claudine's skin was the color of cinnamon and her features were small and attractive. She wore a blue denim dress and a white kerchief bound about her head. Large gold hoops dangled from her pierced ears.

"She'll show you your room," Molly said. "She takes to the stairs better than me." Then she disappeared into the kitchen.

Claudine led the way up the polished wood staircase. At the landing the stairs divided, and each of the two new narrower staircases led up to one wing. Claudine turned to the left and led Kathy down one of two hallways that ran parallel to each other. They met Scott as he came out of Kathy's room.

"I'd like to see you in the study as soon as you freshen up," he told Kathy. "You'll find it downstairs at the back of the house."

Her bedroom was at the center rear of the house—a large airy room with French doors that led out to a wrought-iron balcony overlooking a courtyard. The comfortable-looking double bed had a blue and white striped spread that matched the draperies. A carpet of varied shades of blue covered the floor. The furniture was sturdy and old-fashioned: a dresser with a large mirror, wardrobe, writing table, a nightstand, and rocker. On the nightstand was a kerosene lamp and a

22

white candle in a brass candlestick enclosed in a hurri-
cane shade.

"This is very nice," said Kathy with a feeling of re-
lief. She hadn't known quite what to expect so far out
in the country. No electricity. No phone. Her eyes
searched about questioningly.

"Bathroom across hall," said Claudine, anticipating
her question. "I go now, finish to get dinner ready."

"*Merci.*" After she had gone, Kathy slipped out of
her wrinkled dress and into a brown pleated skirt and
yellow overblouse. She replaced the red jewelry with a
gold medallion on a long chain and gold button earrings. She unhooked the barrette and began brushing
her hair before the mirror. The color of wild honey, it
was parted in the center and feather-cut at the top so
as to form a wave on either side of her forehead. Other
than that, her hair was perfectly straight and reached
almost to her waist. She liked it long. There was so
much she could do with it, different ways to wear it.

She leaned forward to study the oval face looking
back at her from the mirror. Though her eyes were velvety brown, and though she had a pert nose and nice
full lips—put them all together and she was just another pretty girl, in her opinion. You couldn't call her
eyes big or her lashes long, although they were thick.
But her hair—she could not deny its beauty, both in
texture and color. Silky soft, it shone like gold in the
sun. And, of course, in Haiti golden hair was a rarity.
The eyes of everyone she'd met so far had been drawn
to her hair, she couldn't help but notice. It was definitely her most outstanding feature. But with it flowing
about her shoulders, she looked more like a young girl
on holiday than a business person.

She plaited her hair and pinned the two braids
neatly about her head. More dignified. Now she looked
her twenty-one years, she hoped.

She went down to the entry hall and found the
study. The door was open and she stepped over the

23

threshold, the muscles of her stomach tightening nervously.

To her right was a brick fireplace with a painting of Haiti's National Palace centered above it. Books lined the walls on either side of the fireplace, and in front of it stood a large mahogany desk and two armchairs facing each other. The opposite wall contained a couch. All this Kathy took in at a glance.

Her employer stood with his back to her at one of the rear windows, his hands clasped behind him. She coughed discreetly, lingering in the doorway. He had been looking out into the courtyard, and now he turned to face her.

They stared at each other across the room, and she realized she hadn't seen him smile even once. Again that uncomfortable pause.

"Well, come in, come in," he said impatiently. "Don't stand there by the door staring at me as though I had two heads."

She went forward hesitantly, intimidated by his brusque manner. Was this what Mr. Rollet had meant by "temperamental"?

He motioned her to an armchair and moved to the fireplace where he stood contemplating her, leaning against the mantel. His gray eyes looked strangely light against the tanned face and regarded her narrowly, even coldly. Nothing like the thoughtful, dreamy eyes of the photograph, she thought. This was not the same person pictured on the jackets of his books. She felt a pang of disappointment. Where was the sensitivity expressed in that other face? There was a hardness in the set of this man's jaw and in the compressed lips, and the eyes chilled her. She could feel herself squirming inside as he ran his glance over her slim body.

"My sister never mentioned your being so young," he said, frowning. "When she said you were a friend, I took it for granted she was referring to someone within her own age bracket." He made no attempt to hide his displeasure.

"Does it matter . . . as long as I'm competent?" Kathy ventured in a small voice.

"And you're pretty!" He said it like an accusation, ignoring her question.

Astonished by his attitude, she nevertheless felt her pulse quicken. He thought her pretty.

"I don't understand," she faltered. "What does my age or my looks have to do with anything?"

"Plenty, damn it!" he snapped. And he did not bother to offer any explanation.

His unreasonable harshness sent a shock through Kathy. Then came indignation. Famous or not, how dared he treat her so rudely! She rose to her feet. "If you'd like to get someone else . . ." she began stiffly, but he cut her off with an abrupt gesture.

"No time. Besides, a bargain was made, and I never go back on my word."

"Nor I." Her rounded chin went up.

"Well, then, it looks like I'll have to put up with you," he said, running restless fingers through his thick dark hair.

Of all the gall! Her right hand twitched as she fought an urge to slap his arrogant face.

"It looks like we'll have to put up with each other," she countered, for she wasn't quite without a dash of spirit. Angry spots of color flamed in her cheeks, and she met his stare without wavering. When he ordered her to sit down, she did so reluctantly.

He struck a match and lit a cigarette without offering her one, and began pacing the floor, dragging at the cigarette in short puffs, breathing out the smoke with an irascible air. Kathy could see the smooth ripple of muscle in his upper arm each time he raised the cigarette to his lips; and his muscular thighs strained with each step against the fabric of his slim, dark trousers. He looked powerful, restless, angry. Little tremors of nervous reaction ran through her as she watched him, feeling the tension that simmered in his lean, hard body. He had an animal grace, a physical magnetism

25

that disturbed her more than a little, so that when he paused in front of her chair she almost cringed.

"You know shorthand, of course," he shot at her.

She licked her lips nervously. "Of course."

"And you're good at spelling and punctuation? I took Lucy's word for it."

"Yes."

"She said you were familiar with manuscript format. You've worked for other writers?"

"No. Well . . . yes." It was true, after all; she had worked for herself.

The gray eyes probed hers. "Well, which is it—yes or no?"

Her cheeks warmed as she admitted shyly, "I-I write a little myself. Children's stories."

Seeing a sardonic quirk on his lips, she bit her own lest she blurt out the news of her first literary sale. It wouldn't impress a novelist whose literary ventures had reaped incredible returns. To bring up her puny success, and especially now while they were at odds, would only amuse him.

Clasping her hands on her lap, she lowered her lashes and remained silent. She could feel his eyes upon her yet another moment before he turned away and resumed pacing. Evidently he hadn't enough interest to question her about her writing. Either he was too wrapped up in himself, or he thought her a dilettante who scribbled now and then when the mood struck her, nothing important. Well, it *was* important—to her, at least.

She had worked hard over her manuscripts these last three years, even after being in an office all day. Many were the good times she had sacrificed in order to bring to fruition her desire to accomplish something worthwhile in children's literature. Self-taught through trial and error, through studying published stories and reading books on fiction techniques, she finally had come to a point of professionalism that had resulted in her first acceptance with another pending. This had inspired her to revise the best of her stories until they were now as perfect as she could make them.

No, she was no dilettante. She loved the English language, loved arranging words into smooth-flowing sentences. And Mr. Blackburn would soon discover her to be the best assistant he'd ever had.

His curt voice cut into her thoughts. "I expect to have my novel completed by the time school opens in September, typed and ready for my publisher. I'm renting this house here in the mountains so I may have privacy in which to work, free of distractions. I've already spent months on research, even before I came here. The plot is all formed in my mind, so I expect the actual writing to go smoothly. You'll take dictation and type up each day's output so I can see it in print and make any necessary revisions. You will then type the final draft with two carbon copies. Understood?"

She inclined her head, thinking he needn't be so patronizing.

"We breakfast at eight, start work by nine," he went on crisply. "Lunch is at one, dinner at seven. And tea around four o'clock. Molly blows a whistle at mealtimes. You can hear the sound from outside the house, which works well for my son when he's playing outdoors. About your weekends—I'll need you this Saturday, but most often you'll have them free. You might want to ride into Port-au-Prince occasionally when we pick up supplies in the Jeep. And there are horses available out back. I take it your room is satisfactory?"

"Very nice, thank you."

"And the salary suits you?"

"Indeed it's most generous."

"Indeed," sardonically. "That's to compensate for when you get bored or lonely, as you probably will up here." He snubbed out his cigarette in the ashtray on the desk.

I'll have time to work on a new story, she thought. Aloud she said, "I don't think I'll be bored. I enjoy simple things like walking, reading. I'll be glad for a chance to ride, too." She indicated the bookshelves. "May I borrow a book now and then?"

"Feel free. Some belong to the house, some are mine."

A sharp whistle rent the air.

"Ah! Our melodious dinner bell," said Scott, a faint smile softening the chiseled curves of his lips for the first time. Going to the door, he held it open for Kathy. She preceded him out to the hall, suddenly aware she was hungry, and together they entered the dining room, where he seated her to his right.

A few minutes later, young Blackburn joined them with, "Hi! Kathy Miller—right?" He was a wiry lad, brown-toasted by the sun, dressed in tan shirt and shorts, with his face freshly scrubbed and hair neatly combed. Beneath chestnut curls, his blue eyes were alight with interest and curiosity as he looked her over.

Kathy nodded with a smile and offered him her hand as though he were an adult. She had always felt at home with children, and this boy appealed to her at once. "Hi, Tony," she said. She liked the firm way he gripped her hand before sitting down across from her.

Molly brought in the food, which had been cooked by Claudine. They took turns fixing meals, she informed Kathy, so that the household could enjoy native cuisine. Tonight's fare consisted of *grillot*—succulent bits of fried pork that one dipped into a spicy hot sauce—and rice, and sweet potato pudding.

Kathy tasted the pork and exclaimed, "This is delicious."

"So's the sweet potato pudding," said Tony, filling his mouth. "Say, Dad—"

"Not with your mouth full."

He swallowed dutifully. "Marc taught me a new Haitian riddle." And to Kathy, "He's my friend who lives behind the house. Him and his brother Louis. Okay, here's the riddle: *Dé-kwa bwê, dé-kwa mâjé, dé-kwa jété.*"

His father smiled, and Kathy thought what nice

things a smile did for his face. Would that he'd smile at her that way.

"That sounds a bit like French, Tony," she said. "That last word: throw? Throw away?"

"Righto. It's Creole, the native dialect—French and Spanish and African mixed together. Can you translate, Dad?"

"I know little Creole."

"Well, then, here it is in English: Something to drink, something to eat, something to throw away. What is it?"

Both adults pondered the riddle. Scott guessed watermelon. Tony chuckled and shook his head. "You, Miss Miller?"

"Call me Kathy, why don't you."

"Sure, Kathy. Got the answer?"

She wrinkled her brow, pretending deep thought. "Could you give me a hint? I'm not very good at riddles."

"They grow all over Haiti. You must have seen some on the way up here. In tall trees?"

"Coconuts!" It came out of her mouth in a rush that made him laugh, and she saw that his middle front teeth were large. Cute-looking boy. And how relaxed the atmosphere had become since he appeared. She was enjoying the chat around the table, with the soft glow of candlelight on their faces and savory food on their plates. For the moment all was well.

"Here's another," said Tony, showing off with obvious enjoyment. From the way he kept glancing at her, Kathy could tell he was trying to impress her, which she took as a compliment.

"Yo koupé mwê sou-tab, mê yo pa-mâjé mwê," he said. And gave the translation: "They cut me on a table, but they don't eat me."

Silence.

"Aw, Dad, you're not very sharp today. *Kat a-jivé.* Playing cards."

"How simple, once you know the answer," said

29

Kathy, helping herself to more sweet potato pudding. Everything was delicious.

"You've picked up quite a bit of Creole from your playmates, haven't you, son. Too bad it isn't French. You'd have more use for it."

"I'm glad the Buteaus are here, Dad, or who would I play with? They're pretty nice kids. But you know something? They believe in the craziest things—werewolves and evil spirits that can kill and all that kind of junk. Man, I'd be scared to go out the door if I believed in such fairy tales." He turned to Kathy. "Wouldn't you, Miss—Kathy?" She agreed. "Even zombies," he added, stifling a yawn. "Those dumb kids believe in them. Can you imagine?"

"You look tired," said his father, changing the subject abruptly.

"Yeah. I woke up with the rooster this morning. But just a little more pudding, huh?" He helped himself. "Hey, Dad, is Cousin Olivia really coming here to visit us?"

"As far as I know, yes."

"I don't remember her too well. Except the red hair."

He took his time eating the pudding. Then he yawned again, drowsy-eyed, and excused himself from the table. "Night, Kathy. Dad." He went to give his father a hug, and she saw the look of tenderness on the author's face as he tousled the curly hair.

When the youngster had left the room, he said to her, "You'll find that in Haiti most everyone retires early and gets up at dawn. Except when the peasants hold voodoo ceremonies or social dances—usually on Saturday nights, but other times too here in the mountains."

Molly entered to clear the table. "A nice fire in the parlor now," she told them. "I'll bring the coffee there in a few minutes, boss."

"I've told you not to call me that, Molly."

"Yessir, Mr. Blackburn."

The living room had cranberry draperies and a rug to match, and contained a baby grand piano. A sofa and two chairs with clawed feet faced one another before a snappy fire that warmed the damp evening air. Toward the end of dinner it had begun to rain and had grown surprisingly chilly. But, then, they were high up in the mountains, Kathy reminded herself as she chose the chair nearest the flames.

Scott sat opposite her on the sofa, and she found herself watching the firelight reflections play across his face, emphasizing the fine bone structure.

He leaned toward her, hands clasped loosely between his knees. "What Tony said in the dining room, Miss Miller . . . I have no idea how much you know of the occult, but I'd just as soon let him go on thinking the Haitian beliefs are fairy tales. He's too young to be told about the powers of darkness."

"It's not all superstition then?"

"Some of it is, of course. But not all. This truly is the land of the occult. Voodoo works, Miss Miller, which is why Catholicism will never be able to stamp it out."

The Frenchman had said almost the same thing. And now Scott Blackburn, another educated man, was stating that Haiti really *was* weird, that its legends were not merely legends. With all his study and research, he had to know what he was talking about.

"I know what the Bible says concerning the powers of darkness," she said. "But the Haitian beliefs? Zombies, for instance?"

"Now there's a fascinating subject. And I was most skeptical, let me tell you, until I began delving into it and found documented case after case. I went all over, talking personally to many families involved." He shrugged, his lips quirking. "All I have to say is, I can no longer state emphatically that there's no such thing as a zombie. I've begun to think nothing is impossible in this land. Almost."

31

"Really? But you do think some of their beliefs are mere superstition? Like what, for instance."

He thought for a moment. "Haunted mapou trees, in my opinion. That's the cotton tree. They're considered dangerous at night, inhabited by *bacalou*—evil little man-eating demons who carouse inside the huge trunks and feast upon their victims. During the day they rest or wander the countryside in the form of animals, chiefly pigs." His lips twisted wryly. "Should a pig show signs of a personality, it is considered *bacalou* and left to fend for itself."

Kathy smiled. "That does seem a bit hard to swallow," she agreed.

"I've been told," he continued, "that in passing a haunted mapou late at night, one can hear howling and singing and the crunching of bones. Well—feeling foolish, mind you—I listened near a mapou after dark a couple of times and heard nothing. Perhaps when I hear the sounds for myself"—again the wry expression—"I'll be more inclined to believe in *bacalou*."

Kathy giggled. Her host was being congenial, and she was enjoying herself. She liked the sound of his smooth baritone voice, and the more she learned about this strange land, the more interested she became. Perhaps she would write a book of her own about Haiti one day.

Molly appeared with a tray, set it on the coffee table and withdrew. Kathy poured the black Haitian coffee. Tasting hers, she found it strong and delicious, with a marvelous tang to it. She took another experimental sip. It had a smoky flavor that was a bit different from what she was used to. Everything about this country was different, it seemed.

A quiet fell over them as they drank their coffee and gazed into the fireplace where the flames flickered hypnotically. Out of the corner of her eye Kathy saw that Scott's face had turned strangely melancholy, and she wondered if he was thinking of his late wife.

Hoping to draw him away from unhappy recollections, she said, "Mr. Blackburn, tell me more about Haiti. I'm really interested."

His head turned slowly in her direction. "Indeed?" he drawled, and the arrogance was back. The way his eyes flicked across her face made the blood rise to her cheeks; his look seemed to imply she was putting on a pretense for his benefit.

"Had you any interest in this country before you came here?" he asked pointedly.

"Why, I . . . well, no."

"Did you read up on it once you knew you were coming?"

"There wasn't much time—"

"Is there ever enough time?" he interrupted, dismissing her defense with an impatient wave of his hand, as though it were the flimsiest of excuses. "My dear young lady, one must *make* the time." The implication being that since she hadn't, she couldn't be all that interested.

The man was insufferably rude!

He had turned his face away again and was staring into the fire through narrowed eyes. He looked preoccupied, as though he had forgot her presence. She sat there feeling like an admonished child; and when he continued to ignore her, she stood up and said a faint good night. He did not seem to hear or notice when she walked out of the room, and she could not help but feel frustrated.

Had she made a mistake coming here? Like it or not, she was committed for the next several months. She could only hope he wouldn't keep her on the defensive all that time or it was going to be a dreadful summer.

When she had changed into pajamas and brushed her hair, Kathy stepped out through the French doors onto her balcony. It had stopped raining and the stars were out, luminous blossoms against the indigo sky. The wet trees shone darkly, and from the damp earth came pungent jungle odors, strange to her nostrils and

33

faintly disquieting. She could hear tropical tree toads and frogs and cicadas in an evening chorus that was fuller and more varied than at home. Other than that, there were no human sounds, no noises, though it was only nine o'clock. It seemed strange not to hear the hum of cars on a nearby highway.

She closed the doors, blew out the kerosene lamp and crawled between the cool, smooth sheets of her bed. To think that only this morning she had been in the United States, wondering what Haiti was like.

A wave of homesickness swept through her. Home was where loved ones were, people who loved her in return. Here there was no one to care, least of all Scott Blackburn, who had disapproved of her on sight.

I'll show you. I'll do my work so well you'll be glad you hired me.

She closed her eyes and saw his photograph on the screen of her mind. Such a nice photo. Dreamy, thoughtful eyes. Sensitive mouth. No trace of arrogance. Perhaps the trait was not so pronounced at that time. It was an old picture, taken some years before upon publication of his first book, and the same photo had been used on the jacket of his second book. Had success gone to his head so that he was no longer the same person depicted in the photograph? Somehow she felt sure the man in the picture was not the man of today. Pierre Rollet had suggested the loss of his wife might be the cause. But every day there were men who suffered such bereavement without becoming a Jekyll-and-Hyde.

Kathy sighed. If only she'd known he wanted an older person to assist him. If only his sister had known. But phone connections to Haiti were poor, and Mrs. Clark had said that what with noises on the wire and their voices coming through faintly, she had spoken only briefly with her brother.

Well, she was here now and had to make the best of it, and could only hope he too would adjust to the situation. When you couldn't get exactly what you wanted, you took what you could get.

"*C'est la vie*," she whispered, closing her eyes.

She was just dozing off when something brought her upright in bed.

Tom-tom-tomitty-tomitty-tom-tom.

Drums!

She jumped from her bed and on to the balcony again; and she noticed pinpoints of fire flicker on distant hillsides in the velvet darkness of night. The drums echoed across mountains and through valleys like distant thunder. The sound had a deep eerie quality and a primitive beat that pulsated through the air. Kathy could sense the mystery and the drama and the power of Haiti in those drumbeats; they seemed to speak a folk language of their own that could not be put into words.

She remained outside for some minutes, listening intently, trying to pinpoint its direction. One moment the drum talk seemed to come from far off, the next, only a short distance away . . . throbbing . . . throbbing. Voodoo drums.

A tremor went through her. The night suddenly seemed menacing and she quickly retreated into her room, closed the French doors, and locked them.

Chapter Three

Two hours later Kathy was still awake. Sighing, she arose, lit the lamp, and donned her robe and slippers. Perhaps if she read awhile . . .

By the time she realized the study was occupied, her presence was known and she couldn't very well turn tail and run. "I came down to borrow a book," she said from the doorway, the lamp in her hand illuminating her face. "I-I couldn't sleep," she added lamely.

The room was dimly lit by a single lamp on the low table in front of the couch where Scott was seated, fully dressed. He waved her in. "Come, sit a minute."

Thinking he had something to say to her concerning her work, she set down her lamp and sat beside him.

"Drink?" he offered, gesturing toward the decanter on the table.

"No, thank you."

"Oh, come now, this you must try." Apparently he had undergone another mood change and was feeling friendly. He went to a cabinet for an extra glass. "It may help you sleep," he said, giving her a boyish grin as he reseated himself and poured a little into her glass. "Ever taste rum?"

"Only rum cake."

"Well, this is the best—dark gold rum made by the local Barbancourt family. They've been in the business over two hundred years. Anyone who visits Haiti should taste it."

He handed her the glass and refilled his own. "To

your good health, Miss Miller." His went down easily in one gulp.

Kathy took a swallow. It burned going down her throat and made her cough. "I think I'll stick to rum cake," she gasped, setting down the glass.

He laughed, an easy pleasant sound, loosened by the alcohol. "Well, now you can say you've tasted Haiti's famous Rhum Barbancourt. Perhaps you'd prefer sherry?"

"No, no, nothing else."

"Lean back, Miss Miller, relax. You know, your hair is very pretty when it's free like that." And he reached out a hand to stroke it. Then, to her astonishment, he leaned close and peered into her eyes, so close his warm breath fanned her face. "Brown eyes," he murmured. "Nice combination with natural blond hair."

The liquor, she realized, had warmed him into childlike informality. He was relaxed, friendly, but so unlike his reserved self it made her uncomfortable. Conscious of the hour and that she was in her nightclothes, she said, "I'd better get to bed," and made a move to rise—but he caught hold of her wrist and pulled her back down beside him.

"Don't go, Kathy. I could use some company tonight."

He had called her Kathy. She sat there, head lowered, struggling with herself, knowing she should leave yet wanting to stay.

His hand closed over hers, and her heart quickened. And then she saw his mood had changed again. How mercurial he was!

"Do things ever haunt you, Kathy?" There was a slight quiver in his voice. "I keep seeing her . . . all that blood . . ." A dry sob tore from his throat, and he let go her hand.

Her heart melted as she took in the brooding face and anguished eyes. Almost a year, and still he suffered over the untimely death. He must have loved his wife very much. She wondered if he were trying to drown his sorrow in drink and whether he made a habit of it. She wished she could help him, but staying on with him at this time of night seemed improper.

She rose abruptly and moved toward the book-shelves, murmuring, "I did come down for something to read."

"So you did." He came to stand beside her. "Sorry," he said gruffly. "Didn't mean to cry on your shoulder. Want to read up on Haiti? Here . . ." He reached for a volume. "This is a good one." As he handed it to her, their eyes met—locked.

The next moment seemed endless to Kathy, as if time were suspended. She could not release her gaze from his. It was as though some power were pulling her into the liquid depth of his eyes to dissolve her into his very body and make her a part of him. He was a magnet tugging at her, claiming her, weakening her will, and it frightened her. She wanted to run and could not. Even her breath seemed suspended.

The book dropped from her limp fingers as, with a groan, he swept her into his arms and covered her mouth with his. She felt herself go boneless against his muscular body and her arms, almost of their own voli-tion, went up to encircle his neck. Her soft mouth blos-somed beneath his passionate kiss, and she felt her senses spin with excitement and—desire. She should have been repulsed, yet she was not. Stirred to the depths of her being, physically and emotionally, she yearned to soothe and comfort him, ease his hurt and loneliness.

And then, roughly, shockingly, he thrust her from him. She saw the muscles of his jaws tighten as he stared down into her face; a pulse beat at his temple.

"Go upstairs, for the love of God!" he said in a harsh voice. And deliberately turned his back on her.

Numbly, Kathy stumbled from the room, overcome with shame as she realized he regretted the kiss. It meant nothing to him and could have happened with any girl. He was making that clear to her.

With fire in her cheeks, and feeling cheapened, she ran up the stairs to her bedroom. If only she hadn't permitted her emotions to rule her head! Time had not yet dimmed the pain of his wife's death, and he was far from ready to give his heart to another woman. He was still in love with his wife, with the memory of her. This, then, was why he had wanted an older assistant—so as not to become romantically involved. And she had succumbed like a quivering jellyfish the moment he touched her.

She flung herself on her bed and pressed her burning face into the pillow. When, finally, she got her emotions under control, she gave herself a stern lecture. She must gather her tattered pride about her and play it cool, hold up her head and show that man he needn't fear she was going to fall all over him because of what happened. In fact, she told herself, she must act like it never happened. That would convey it meant no more to her than it did to him.

Morning sunlight played over Kathy's golden hair and across her face; that and the sound of children's voices nudged her awake. Lifting heavy lids, she squinted at her clock on the nightstand and saw it was almost seven o'clock. She pushed down the button of the alarm, which hadn't gone off yet, and wished she could remain in bed. Her head felt heavy, her body weary.

And then, recalling last night's humiliation, she groaned aloud and turned her face into the pillow. How could she face her employer so soon after that hurtful scene!

She toyed with the idea of playing sick. But that was dishonest. Besides, to be absent would attach too much importance to what had happened. No, she couldn't crawl into a corner and hide because she had been wounded. She had to put on a bold face and go on with whatever remnants of pride she had left.

Her limbs felt like lead after an almost sleepless night, and it was an effort to crawl out of bed. She shrugged into her robe and slippers and crossed the room to the French doors. How nice to have a balcony. Stepping outside, she saw remnants of morning fog. But the sun was out, for dawn broke early in the tropics, and the mist dissipated even as she watched.

The unpaved courtyard below was the width of the house and twice as long, enclosed on both sides by stone walls. The rear entrance to the yard was an open space with crumbling posts that once held a gate. An oak tree grew near the house, providing shade, and she could see a swing suspended from one of the limbs. There was a chill in the morning air, and Tony and Claudine's sons were playing catch in the sunshine, laughing and poking fun whenever one of them fumbled the ball.

At the end of the courtyard to her left, Kathy could see a long, low wooden building with two sets of double doors. The horses probably were stabled there. A little thatched-roof cottage and produce garden stood outside the courtyard a short distance away. She could see a man moving about. Claudine's husband, no doubt. She detected the pungent odor of an outdoor charcoal fire mingled with the delicious aroma of strong coffee. She took a deep breath. How good they smelled, the coffee and the burning coals.

The children were partly hidden from Kathy's view by a limb of the tree, and were unaware of her watching them play. As laughter burst from their lips a door downstairs squeaked open and Molly came storming out carrying a long wooden spoon.

"Children! Everybody's not awake yet. Hush, or I be paddling you, all three of you. Go play outside the yard, Tony, till breakfast be ready. Scoot!" She brandished the spoon as though it were a sword. The boys obeyed while snickering at her theatrics, and Tony threw a comment over his shoulder about it being time for all good people to rise and shine. As if to confirm his opinion, a cock crowed lustily from the vicinity of the cottage.

Kathy withdrew from the balcony, made the bed, and went across the hall to the bathroom. Finding only cold water, she washed quickly and returned to her room to don a white linen blouse and her brown skirt. A little powder and lipstick, a few twists of her hair into a loose bun, like Molly's, on the nape of her neck and she was ready. Now downstairs for an early cup of coffee to bolster her courage.

She could hear Molly talking to someone as she approached the kitchen, and she tapped on the open door before stepping inside. It was a large room with yellow curtains at the double windows. Underneath was a wooden sink with a hand-operated pump. An old gas refrigerator hummed near a black wood-burning stove. Molly was just pouring herself a cup of coffee from a big percolator.

"Good morning," said Kathy. "I thought I heard you talking to someone."

"To myself why shouldn't I talk?" Molly chuckled. "At least I'll know somebody's listening."

Kathy smiled. "Never thought of it that way."

The housekeeper seemed glad to see her and quickly brought out another cup. They sat down together at the big table in the center of the room.

"I love Haitian coffee," Molly confided. "I'll miss it when we leave here."

Kathy took a swallow and decided the burnt flavor was what made it distinctive. Each time she drank it she liked it better. Glancing about the kitchen, she remarked wryly, "Bet I know what you won't miss."

"That blasted wood stove and the water pump, for sure. As for hot water, that we got to heat on the stove, and never enough it be. I tell you, lass, I can't wait to get home to California."

"What do you do here in your spare time, Molly?"

"Brung my knitting along, and some paperback novels."

"Tell me about the Buteau family. I saw their cot-

41

tage from my balcony. Claudine's husband—what's his name?"

"Fernand. They raise vegetables for themselves and to sell at market, and they're caretakers for this house. Mr. Blackburn pays them for any extra chores, of course, like bringing wood for the fires or driving down to the city on errands. Fernand loves driving the Jeep. Belongs to the estate, it does. And the horses, too."

"This is an awfully large house for a summer place, isn't it?"

" 'Tain't just a summer place. The Devereaux family live here all year round. But they are spending this summer in France with relatives, as I understand it, so they put it up for rent. Finished your coffee? I'll be glad to show you this part of the house, if you like. Won't take but a few minutes, and I already got my muffin batter mixed."

On one side of the kitchen was a walk-in pantry that led directly into the front dining room; on the kitchen's other side at the rear left corner of the house was the laundry, with a door exiting to a narrow back hall that split off from the front hall. From here one could go out into the courtyard. Directly across this back hall was Molly's room, beneath Kathy's; and on the other side of her room was another hall that led to the study situated at the rear right corner of the house. Between the study and the living room was a bathroom.

The house had three bathrooms, Molly informed Kathy, and some twelve rooms, not counting storage, laundry, and pantry. The family that owned it must be a large one, but why anybody would want to dwell full time so far up the mountain was beyond Molly's comprehension. With no telephone or electricity or hot water heater, one might as well be living back in olden times.

She returned to the kitchen to prepare breakfast, and Kathy went to glance over the books in the study. There were works on philosophy, English drama, Haiti. And some novels. Also volumes written in French. On

42

a bottom shelf lay American newspapers and several copies of the *Reader's Digest*.

She pulled out a book entitled *Papa Doc* and sat down to glance through it. One interesting paragraph stated that Haitian peasants were convinced voodoo charms could cause sickness and even death. It sounded like an old wives' tale. Still, her employer had said almost anything was possible in this land of the occult.

Hearing the breakfast whistle, she finished the page and replaced the volume on the shelf.

She met Molly coming out of the kitchen with a tray containing only a huge mug of steaming black coffee. Evidently Scott Blackburn had a hangover to contend with.

"Tony's at table already," Molly told her. "You two go on and eat. The boss will be down later."

Tony greeted her cheerfully as she entered the dining room; and it pleased her that he got up and seated her, as his father would do. A well-trained youngster.

"Molly doesn't believe in three squares a day and tea besides," he informed her as he helped himself to a blueberry muffin. "Oh, well, a skinny breakfast means a fat lunch. We don't have to wait for Dad, he's got a headache. Guess he won't be doing his exercises this morning."

Kathy poured her coffee. She said carefully, "Does he get them often?"

"Now and then. When he can't sleep at night."

"Has he tried sedatives?"

"You mean sleeping pills? They don't always work."

She broke off a piece of muffin and carried it to her lips.

"How long have you been in Haiti?" she asked him.

"Oh, 'bout three months. Since March."

"Like it?"

"It's okay. Some things I like, some I don't. I'd rather be home, but not without my dad."

"What about school?"

"Well, Dad wanted me to join him at vacation

43

time"—he grinned impishly—"but I fussed until he agreed to bring me along with him. He's been tutoring me himself. Now I'm on vacation."

"I like your housekeeper," she said.

"Yeah, Molly's okay. Been with us a long time." He said nothing about his mother, and Kathy thought it wiser not to bring up the subject.

When they had finished eating, she suggested they go see what his friends were up to. She could hear a pounding in the distance. "I've got time to spare," she said. "By the way, think your dad will be up to working this morning?"

"He wouldn't let anything keep him from writing his book. But I wish those headaches would go away and stay away. He never used to get them."

"Let's hope time will cure them." It was all she could think to say to him.

Using the rear exit, they went first to the long wooden building in the courtyard so Tony could show her the horses. He swung open the double doors on the left. Walking in on the dirt floor, she saw a dun and a bay munching hay in separate stalls. At the other end of the building stood the Jeep. There were bags of feed piled in a corner, and tools, and an old-fashioned lawn mower. On a long wall rack were some folded blankets, a couple of saddles and bridles, and other paraphernalia.

From there they headed for the Buteau cottage, and the sound of wood against wood grew louder as they neared it. Claudine's husband was outside pulverizing grain in a large, crude mortar. One of his sons was tossing feed to the chickens in a wire enclosure, and the other was busy grooming a burro with a stiff brush. Both boys paused in their work to stare at Kathy. A goat and several pigs ambled about; and as one of the pigs headed for the garden where neat rows of vegetables flourished, Tony chased after it with a shout.

"Good morning," Kathy said to the man. She received an instant smile that was dazzling white against

44

his ebony skin. "I'm Kathy Miller. You must be Fernand." She peered into the mortar, a tall hollowed-out section of log standing on end. "Is this how you make meal?"

"*Oui*, mam'selle." He wiped his sweating face and took a break, laying his pestle across the top of the mortar. He had on denim workclothes and looked strong and muscular.

"Where's Claudine?" She glanced toward the open door of the cottage.

"Friday be market day in Kenscoff. Claudine take vegetables to sell dere," he said in a deep rich voice that made her think of thick chocolate syrup.

"Fernand, with a voice like that, I'll bet you're a fine singer."

He beamed at the compliment. And when she asked to see his house, he ushered her in cordially and with pride drew her attention to the wooden floor. On her way up the mountain she had glanced into many open doorways and had noticed that the floors were of hard-packed earth. This hut was larger than most and the plaster walls had a clean whitewashed look. A handmade table and chairs and a cupboard seemed to be the only furniture. Stacked in one corner were sleeping mats made of banana fronds.

Then Kathy noticed a little table covered with a white cloth next to the doorway. On the wall above it were displayed pictures of saints, with one of St. Patrick given predominance in the center. A lamp burned on the table, fashioned from half a coconut shell and containing oil with a wick floating above two splinters of bone arranged in a cross. A perpetual lamp, probably.

"I see you've placed Saint Patrick's picture in the center," she said to Fernand. "Is he your patron saint?"

"Him Damballah, de root-*loa* of my family."

"Damballah? Oh, yes, the snake god." A voodoo shrine. Of course. Yet hardly distinguishable from a

45

Catholic shrine. Not being Catholic herself, Kathy had to stop and think—wasn't St. Patrick supposed to have driven the snakes out of Ireland? What with there being snakes in his lithograph, it was no wonder he represented Damballah to the voodooist. Root-*loa*, she decided, must mean patron spirit or god, and Damballah was the protector of this particular household.

Seeing two dark green bottles sealed with corks on the table, she asked their purpose.

"Dey contain de souls of my sons," Fernand told her solemnly. His accent was more pronounced than that of his wife.

Kathy tried to conceal her dismay. "Why in bottles, Fernand? How can a person live without his soul?"

"You not know dere be two souls in de head? One big, one little. Only de big are in de bottles. Marc and Louis still have one soul each in de head." He patted one of the bottles reverently. "Bottle is to protect. *Houngan* make special ceremony. No evil spell can hurt my boys while der soul are safe in de bottles."

Kathy wondered if he had considered the possibility of the bottles breaking or falling into the wrong hands.

She glanced at her watch. "I've got to get to work now. I'll visit Claudine another time."

He nodded and smiled his broad friendly smile and went back to pounding grain. The sound cut through the air; she could hear it all the way to the house. Such labor for the bare necessities of life, she reflected soberly, for things she merely lifted off supermarket shelves back home. She could just imagine how bug-eyed would be Fernand's reaction to the enormous variety of packaged goods she had always taken for granted. How few and simple were the wants of the Haitians compared to her fellow Americans, so blessed with abundance as to take even luxuries for granted.

She hesitated in the hall as she heard a drawer being opened in the study. Scott was in there, all right. That big mug of coffee must have helped.

Remember, Kathy—as though nothing happened last night.

She took a deep breath and walked in. "Good morning." She managed to keep her voice cool and unemotional.

"Morning." He was rummaging in one of the desk drawers and did not glance up. He looked a bit pale, she noted, but otherwise normal—sober, clean shaven, and immaculate in coordinating dark green shirt and slacks.

She seated herself in one of the chairs facing him. "I just met Fernand. We had an interesting talk," she said, making casual conversation to fill the silence and to indicate last night was forgotten already. "He showed me the family shrine. Did you know he keeps souls in bottles?"

He straightened up and met her glance. "Miss Miller," he began, "about last night . . . well, I owe you an apology. I wasn't myself."

She waved a hand airily. "I know. And we both got carried away for a moment. Let's forget it, shall we?" She marveled at the lightness of her tone and congratulated herself for carrying it off so well. He'd never guess how much he had hurt her.

Looking relieved, he said, "Well, then, let's begin our work. Oh, by the way, do you drive with a stick shift? Ever handle anything like a Jeep?"

"At home I drive a Volkswagen with a stick shift," she told him. "And I've handled a car with four-wheel drive once or twice."

"Good. Molly needs to get out of the house once in a while, and she'd like to visit the Kenscoff market after lunch. I'll show you how to run the Jeep. You might enjoy the outing. Frankly, I don't feel up to it."

"You mean I'm to take off from work?"

"Nine to one each day should suffice, Miss Miller. Unless you need more time to transcribe your notes. And, occasionally, I may call on you at odd times. All in all, I don't think you'll find yourself overworked."

"Anything I can do, any time, please let me know," she said fervently. "I want to earn my salary—"

He cut her off with that air of impatience. "You'll earn it if you do a good job. It's not the number of hours you put in that concerns me. It's the quality of your work—neatness, good paragraphing and punctuation, proper setup of dialogue, and so forth. Now, about your salary, how do you want it?"

She asked him to send most of it by check to her bank at home and give her the rest in cash. And could she take the Jeep out on her own once in a while?

He assented, though reluctantly. "As long as you let me know ahead of time. Frankly, I'd rather you didn't go about often by yourself. I don't mean you wouldn't be safe," he added. "You can walk through any area of the capital without fear, even at night. But there's always the possibility of car trouble."

He handed her a pad and pencil, and they went to work.

After a couple of hours dictating at a pace that was comfortable for her, he said, "I'll let you get to your typing now. Leave the pages on the desk and I'll go over them later. About the final draft—wait till each chapter is finished in case any changes occur to me."

As she typed up her notes—and she could tell already it was to be a romance with political overtones—Kathy marveled that she'd have so much free time. This was really an ideal job. Not only interesting, but educational. By the time the assignment was over she'd be well-versed on Haiti.

Tony went along to Kenscoff with the women. Once they arrived at the native market, Kathy was glad she had come and that she had brought her camera. It was a picturesque scene. The merchants, mostly women, were either bargaining with customers or happily swapping gossip among themselves, while their children played nearby. Kathy spied Claudine and waved to her, and she waved back gaily. The atmosphere seemed one of festivity. Old men played dominoes on the side of the road around tables laid with checkerboard cloths. Ragged little urchins pursued the tourists, offering flowers, hoping for a coin. One little boy dogged Kathy's footsteps until she rewarded him with a second dime for sheer perseverance.

The place was alive with people, goats, calves, donkeys, dogs—many voices, much laughter. There were fruits and vegetables of every variety, mahogany carvings, colorful native paintings, handwoven goods of straw, and much more, including hand-embroidered shirts hung from trees. Kathy selected a shirt for herself and, because Tony advised her bargaining was expected of her, managed to get it for four dollars and some straw sandals for one dollar. Then she spied some native necklaces and picked up half a dozen for another dollar. Created from natural brown seeds intermingled with brightly painted seeds, they would make nice gifts for friends.

"Tony, let me buy you something. What would you like?"

He selected a pair of gourd maracas, painted with bright designs and shiny with varnish—only seventy-five cents.

What prices, marveled Kathy. It was a shopper's paradise, and one could easily succumb to an endless buying spree if one weren't careful. She would have liked to purchase more, except that she had promised to patronize Mr. Rollet's shop. As for Molly, she limited herself to a sisal tote bag and sandals.

It wasn't until she had taken several snapshots that Kathy realized she was expected to pay for the privilege of photographing the natives. Their eager outstretched hands brought it plainly to her attention. Tony advised her small change would do, and he distributed it for her.

One highlight of Kenscoff was the Châtelet des Fleurs, with its acres and acres of sweet peas and other flowers grown for air shipment to the United States market. Kathy found the floral display enchanting. All in all, this day she had dreaded facing was turning out to be a pleasant one.

That evening Tony asked his father just when their visitor was coming.

"June twenty-seventh," Scott told him. Then he turned to Kathy. "Olivia is a distant cousin who's been living in Italy these last half dozen years. She married an Italian industrialist from Milan named Borelli, but I gather the marriage was a stormy one. They were divorced recently. She plans on coming to Haiti and wants to spend a couple of weeks in the mountains with us." He shrugged carelessly. "I was surprised to hear from her after so long, but we've plenty of room, and I've always found her interesting. We were raised in the same home town, and she often brought her problems to me."

"I bet she had—" Kathy caught herself. Then, as he eyed her expectantly, she said with a little laugh, "Just a silly remark. I was going to say I bet she had a crush on you when the two of you were growing up."

He cocked a quizzical eyebrow at her. "And what makes you think that? Actually, it was the other way around. She was beautiful even in her teens, but she never looked upon me as a romantic prospect. I wasn't much to look at in those days. Then I went away to college and by the time I saw her again, I was married and had a son."

And now you're free and she's free.

Kathy found the thought oddly depressing.

Chapter Four

Saturday morning began well. Scott—she was beginning to think of him by his given name—appeared at table with a benign expression on his face. He smelled of after-shave lotion, and his knitted white shirt emphasized the deep tan of his skin. He actually smiled at her as he took his place at the head of the table.

"All set to help me out this morning, Miss Miller?"

"Ready to go."

"I see you're wearing a dress. Bring any slacks?"

She eyed him uncertainly. "Several pairs, as a matter of fact."

"Change after breakfast," he ordered. And at her puzzled look, "We'll be working on the floor."

"The floor?" she echoed.

"I've accumulated numerous notes, and we'll have to separate them according to subject. Might as well get that done before we go any further into the book. I thought it'd be easier to just sit on the rug and spread them out in front of us. More room. There's quite a stack."

"Oh, I see." It sounded very informal, almost fun.

Molly came pushing a loaded serving cart through the swinging door of the pantry.

"Ah, pancakes!" said Tony happily. "Hope you made a hundred, Molly. I'm hungry hungry hungry."

"Not quite a hundred, love. And when are you not hungry hungry hungry? Must be the mountain air. But for Molly—well, I be skipping breakfast, or I'll never be getting my wish."

"What's that?" asked Tony.

"To be weighed and found wanting," she said with a straight face. She transferred everything from the cart to the table, and left the room muttering that the novel should be finished in record time so they could all get back to civilization.

"Poor Molly," Scott commented dryly. "I imagine she'll appreciate our modern kitchen like never before after tackling this one."

Her gray head came poking round the pantry door. "And right you are, Mr. Blackburn, sir. You know the first thing I'll do when we get home? Shine up my gorgeous electric stove and cook up something extra special. You can bet on it." She let the door swing shut, carrying on a running dialogue with herself.

Tony consumed three large pancakes topped with honey, and several sausages, as well as all his juice and milk. "I ate as much as you, Dad," he boasted, patting his stomach contentedly.

Scott reached over to tweak his nose. "Do you know you've grown an inch since we arrived here? This mountain air does agree with you. Now, what's on your agenda for this morning?"

"Thought I'd help the Buteaus weed the garden. Then we're going swimming. We've got a great place for swimming, Kathy. There's even a waterfall."

"Just don't let me catch you going alone or you'll be grounded in the yard for a full week," his father warned. "And stay away from the falls."

They bantered back and forth for a few moments, and then Tony left. Scott offered Kathy a cigarette, and she told him she didn't smoke. He lit one for himself and said, "How would you like to see a voodoo ceremony on Saturday night? Not tonight, next Saturday."

"You mean it?"

"Certainly I mean it. I've made friends with a *houngan* near Furcy and have attended a couple of his ceremonies. I'll expect you to take mental notes, of course, and get them down on paper later."

"Should be interesting," she murmured.

"Very." He looked amused. "Now get into those slacks." He glanced at his wristwatch. "I'll see you in the study at nine, and be prompt." His requests sounded like commands, but since he was in a pleasant mood, Kathy didn't mind.

They left the dining room together, and he headed for the study, while she went upstairs to change her clothes.

He was seated Indian fashion on the floor of the study between two piles of index cards when she walked in. On the rug in front of him other cards were laid out neatly in horizontal rows. He patted the place beside him. "Sit here, Miss Miller, next to these notes."

She made herself comfortable with her legs drawn up under her. Glancing at the cards laid out in rows before them, she saw that he had printed a subject on each one. Set in alphabetical order, the top row began with ART and the bottom row ended with ZOMBIES.

"Can you read my handwriting?" he asked, indicating her stack of cards. She looked over one and nodded. "You're going to have to skim each card and lay it beneath the proper subject heading. I'll do the same with my bunch. When we're done, each subject pile will go into separate envelopes so I can look up things as needed."

Apparently he preferred index cards to notebooks. Less bulky, she thought, and could easily be carried in a pocket.

She found it required considerable stretching to reach some of the subject headings. Even Scott had to stretch, and once when he leaned toward the right at the same time that she leaned toward the left, their cheeks brushed lightly.

She turned her head away as a heat wave washed up to flood her face with color. Slight as the contact had been, it quickened the beat of her heart. What was the matter with her, that this man should affect her so? If this was what the television commercials referred to as sex appeal, Scott Blackburn had more than his share.

She kept her eyes averted, though she could not help but be sensitive to his nearness after that. When she dared steal a glance at him from beneath her lashes, she saw he was concentrating on his work, oblivious to the turmoil going on inside her.

Being unfamiliar with his notes, it took Kathy longer than it did Scott to appraise the cards according to subject matter. His pile done, he fetched a clipboard, a stack of legal-size envelopes, and a pen, and began printing the subject headings on the envelopes.

"There. I'm done," said Kathy.

Together, they filled the envelopes and placed them in a bottom drawer of the desk.

Kathy glanced at her wristwatch and saw it was quarter to one. The bending and stretching had fatigued her. Even Scott looked tired, for he'd been at it longer than she. He took a deep breath and stretched himself. She saw him wince. He undid the top button of his knitted shirt and slipped in a hand to gingerly feel the back of one shoulder. "Feels all knotted," he said with a grimace. "Think I'll lie down after lunch."

Kathy pulled out the desk chair. "Sit here," she heard herself say briskly. "No use lying down with bunched-up muscles. You'll not rest. Let me fix them for you."

"Are you a masseuse?"

"Not really . . ." Her voice was beginning to falter. Did he think her brazen? "My dad before he died was a bookkeeper, and I used to—he thought I had a knack for it. It won't take but a few minutes."

Scott was eying her with raised eyebrows. Squeezing the base of his neck, he succeeded only in causing himself pain. "Damnation!" he muttered.

"You have to sort of knead it," Kathy told him. "May I try?"

"What have I got to lose." He eased into the chair. "It's damned uncomfortable."

Standing behind him, she placed her fingertips on either side at the base of his neck. *Be still, my heart.* She could feel the knotted muscles beneath the warm skin and began working them gently with circular motions, knowing it would hurt at first.

Within minutes, he relaxed beneath her hands, and she could feel the tense muscles loosening. She loved making people comfortable and might have leaned toward a nursing career had she not had literary aspirations.

"That's enough," he said suddenly. And stood up. "Fine. Thanks." He spoke without looking at her, and she sensed at once that he had withdrawn into a shell. Was it because of her touch?

"I hope it helped," she said lamely.

He nodded and went to a window to stand looking out silently, his back to her. She stood by the desk, not knowing quite what to do, and was relieved to hear Molly's whistle summoning them to the dining room.

It was a light lunch: vegetable soup with rolls and butter, finger bananas, and coconut milk. Tony appeared with his hair curling in damp little tendrils, and Scott patted him on the head. "How was the swim?"

"Good. Why don't we all go next time? You and me and Kathy." Kathy was touched that he included her, as though she were a member of the family.

"We'll see." Scott ladled soup into their bowls. "Eat up. Then I think you ought to rest for an hour, son. You've been on the go since early morning."

There was little talk after that, and when the meal was over they retired to their respective rooms.

Kathy decided to start a new story that had been simmering in her mind. She knew the beginning and the end. And the title: *The Juggler.* Perhaps if she wrote down the introduction, the rest would follow. With pencil and paper, she sat down at the writing table and began. Based on the art of juggling, her tale concerned a lad and his dad who ran a service station and general store out West. The boy liked to juggle

55

with the apples, potatoes, and onions, much to the annoyance of his father, who wanted him to work more and play less.

She filled one sheet of paper and felt a twinge at the back of her neck. Though she'd had a good night's sleep, all that neck bending and arm stretching in the office had put a strain on her muscles. And here she was bending her neck again. Perhaps she'd better put the writing aside for now and lie down before *her* muscles became knotted. Besides, she wasn't sure how to proceed with the story.

It was the first time she'd had a double bed all to herself and she stretched her limbs luxuriously. *I bet Scott has a king-size bed at home,* she thought. No doubt he lived in a big, beautiful house—near San Francisco, wasn't it?

Let's see . . . the story . . . should the father forbid Timmy from juggling at all? Should Timmy disobey, to add to the conflict? Suppose . . .

She woke up half an hour later and went straight to the writing table while the dream fragment was fresh in her mind. She had no sooner got it down, than there came a soft, hesitant tap-tap on her door. She went to open it. It was Tony.

"I didn't wake you, did I?" he said. "I wasn't going to knock again, in case you were sleeping."

"I was awake. Come on in. Had your nap?"

"Yup." He stepped over the threshold. "Thought maybe you'd go riding with me. I want to show you our swimming place. You'll like it, it's great. Ever been on a horse?"

"A couple of times. Where are your friends?"

"They been working in the garden again and just went in to lie down. Everybody's resting. Even Molly."

"And you're all alone?" She glanced toward the table. "I was working on something."

"Aw, Kathy, come?"

"Well . . ." She tweaked his nose gently. "On one condition."

"What's that?"

"Say pretty please," she teased.

He laughed. "Silly! Okay—pretty please, pretty please. Now you have to come." She felt rewarded by his happy grin.

They went to the outbuilding and saddled the horses, and set out at a walking pace toward the front of the house. From the road that went down to Furcy a beaten path curved sharply to the right between a line of trees. As they followed it, Kathy realized it was making a wide U-turn back the way they had come. Soon they had passed the house again as they climbed upward; she caught a glimpse of its roof in the distance.

Soon she could hear the waterfall. They reached a level plateau, and there it was—a cascade of water plunging down the side of the stone cliff. It splashed into a large oval pool some forty feet below. There was a clump of willows at the water's edge, and all around was lush greenery with a sprinkling of wildflowers.

"Oh, Tony, what a beautiful spot!" cried Kathy, enchanted. "If I were an artist, I'd surely want to paint it. I must bring my camera next time we come here."

They dismounted and let the horses drink, then tied them to some shrubbery. Tony spread out a blanket he had brought along for them to sit on.

"Is it deep?" Kathy asked, raising her voice so as to be heard over the rushing falls. She picked up a pebble and tossed it into the pool and watched it make ripples.

"Not very. Only under the waterfall."

She watched the falls plummet forcefully down the high stone cliff on the left, and beat and foam upon the boulders at its base. Their tops were worn smooth from the constant pummeling.

"This is where the Buteaus get their drinking water and bathe," Tony informed her. He pointed to where the pool's excess water flowed into a stream that wound off into the forest. "That's where Claudine washes her clothes. The water stays clean 'cause it's always moving."

"Did you figure that out for yourself?"

"Well . . ." He grinned sheepishly. "Dad mentioned it."

Leaning over impulsively, she kissed the top of his head. "Never mind. I think you're unusually bright."

He did not reply, and she could see his cheeks reddening. He turned his head away, suddenly shy, and began plucking the flowers surrounding their blanket.

A rush of tenderness filled Kathy's heart. Beneath the chestnut curls the nape of his neck appeared so young, so vulnerable. Poor child, to have lost his mother so early in life. He was fortunate to have Molly, of course, but a youngster that age still needed his mother's love and attention. He missed her keenly —Kathy surmised this because although he was outgoing and talkative, he had not mentioned her. It hurt too much.

"I think we'd better get back now," she said after a while, getting to her feet.

He stood up and silently handed her the bouquet of wildflowers he had gathered, tied together with a stem.

"Why, thank you, dear. They'll look nice in my room." She went to tuck the stems under her saddle while Tony folded the blanket.

On their way back down the trail, he drew up his mount and pointed to their left where a narrow path led into the pine and hardwood forest. "Somebody lives there, I think. Let's take a look, shall we? There's time before tea."

They entered the forest single file, his smaller dun-colored horse in the lead. Tall trees interlaced overhead so that the sun filtered through only in small patterns. It was very cool here.

The path led them to a hut set beneath a mahogany tree. The door was open. They dismounted and looked inside. It appeared to be some kind of temple. Seeing no one, and drawn by curiosity, they went in. Tony wrinkled his nose in distaste.

"Stinks," he announced unnecessarily. It was a strange, moldy odor—the smell of damp earth and wood too long away from the purifying effects of sunlight.

Against the wall opposite the door was a large cement cube that reminded Kathy of an old-fashioned masonry oven. The recess in front held plates of food, and on top stood a conglomeration of things: candles, incense, clay pots, a liquor bottle, a rattle, a bell, and more.

It occurred to her this must be a voodoo altar, and the plates of food in the recess were offerings to some god or gods.

She edged toward the doorway, "Let's get out of here, Tony," she whispered. There was something about this place, a strangely disquieting atmosphere that made her long to be out in the sunlight.

"In a minute." Tony had picked up one of the clay pots and was lifting the lid to look inside. Somehow the sight of it in his hand panicked Kathy, though she didn't know why.

"Put that down!" she ordered, her voice so sharp it startled him, causing his hand to jerk. The pot hit the concrete altar and fell to the ground in pieces, along with its contents: several tarnished coins, some beads, and other small items Kathy could not identify.

He laid the lid on the altar. "Why d'you have to startle me like that? It was just an old pot."

Was it? If this was a voodoo temple, it was possible they had committed a sacrilege in breaking the clay pot.

"Let's go," she said again, striving to conceal her anxiety.

They paused outside the doorway. A tall, dark-skinned native woman stood before the hut watching them with arms folded across her chest. She wore a brown Mother Hubbard and a red cloth bound about

59

her head. Her eyes, staring at them from above high cheekbones, were opaque and unreadable, her face an expressionless mask.

Kathy felt the skin prickle along the back of her neck, as though cold fingers were touching her. Though the woman did not speak or move, her hostility was like a living force. They had trespassed.

As they mounted their horses and turned away, Kathy could feel those hard black eyes boring into her back until they were out of sight. Neither she nor Tony spoke until they had left the forest. Then he said, "That was a *mambo*. A voodoo priestess."

"How do you know?"

"Fernand told us boys about her," he confessed. "I wanted to get a look at her voodoo altar. They say she practices black magic. Fernand says all voodoo priests know how to cook up black magic against their enemies, but most of them don't 'cause it's dangerous. They'd have to make a pact with the devil before they could put a curse on someone." He snorted. "I don't believe it, do you? Still, I didn't like that woman."

Kathy made her tone light as she said, "Oh, well, forget her. We'll probably never see her again. And stay away from that temple."

"We won't mention we went there, okay? Dad might not like it."

"I'd just as soon he not know," she said.

The stony eyes of that woman . . . A person with eyes like that would fear nothing, not the devil himself. Again she felt a prickling sensation across the back of her neck.

Deliver me, Lord, from meeting up with HER again.

Chapter Five

They were in time for tea on the patio outside the French doors of the dining room. Paved with old bricks, the patio held a grouping of outdoor furniture. Scott was stretched out on a chaise longue, reading, and Molly was setting the tea things on a round, white wrought-iron table. He stood up as Kathy appeared.

"I showed Kathy our swimming place," Tony said, as they were seated.

"Beautiful spot for a picnic," Kathy murmured, not quite meeting Scott's eyes. "I'll pour the tea, Molly."

It was silly to let the forest incident upset her, she told herself as she filled the cups. The clay pot could be replaced. Still, she wished she knew its purpose.

There was bread and butter and juicy pink mangoes already peeled and cut. It was Kathy's first taste of mangoes. "It reminds me of peaches," she said, "only better. No—pineapple, I think. Or is it both? My, what I've been missing." And she popped another sweet, succulent piece into her mouth.

After tea, Scott went into the living room; and when Kathy heard him playing the piano, she went in to listen. With fairly good technique he ran through an old Beatles tune and a Strauss waltz.

She applauded. "Oh, I wish I could play an instrument!"

"You should hear Olivia play," he said, leaving the piano bench to sit with her. "And sing. She does everything remarkably well." And as he went on about her, she sounded so bright and talented, Kathy wished he'd change the subject. Too bad she was a *distant* cousin, she found herself thinking.

When he went outside to play horseshoes with Tony, she paused to wonder if she was jealous, and bit her lip, frowning. Why would she be jealous? She was nothing to Scott other than a temporary employee. And he was nothing to her.

She began pacing the floor. "He's nothing to me," she whispered. And repeated it, "Nothing. Just my boss."

So what was she uptight about? It was ridiculous. She'd only known the man a couple of days.

She went to the study for the envelope marked VOODOO. There among the cards she found one that seemed to answer the question persisting in the back of her mind. Skimming through it, she read:

> . . . One item of particular interest on the voodoo altar is the *pot tête*—head pot. Such pots, often of clay, are used to contain spirits. Each person, it is believed, carries a spirit in his head during his lifetime. When he dies, there's a ceremony to remove the spirit so it will not go "below the water" with the one who died. The *houngan* helps the spirit enter the head pot.
>
> When one is initiated into the *vaudou*, he receives a *pot tête* of his own. Into it go sacrificial articles, and he must keep the pot until he dies.

Kathy shivered as she replaced the card in the envelope. So! She had caused Tony to break a head pot, a sacred voodoo vessel.

Oh, come now, she reasoned with herself, *you know you don't believe in such nonsense. It's just one of their superstitions, like the man-eating bacalou.*

Still, it wasn't important what *she* believed. To the *mambo* the head pot had special significance. Suppose she held the breakage against them and sought revenge? No! She mustn't think like that or she'd turn into a nervous wreck.

Hearing the clink of horseshoes from outside and Tony's excited squeals as he gained some points, she looked out the window. The Buteau brothers had joined him and his father as partners in the game.

She got her camera and went outside to take pictures. They all wore shorts, and the fuzz on Scott's muscular legs was bleached halfway blond by the tropical sun. Tony took time to introduce his friends to her. Marc, the older boy, was eleven and resembled Claudine both in complexion and facial features. Louis was nine, a miniature of his father. He seemed fascinated by Kathy's hair, which she had loosened. Murmuring something in Creole, he reached up a hand to caress the shining locks.

"He thinks your hair is real gold," said Tony with a grin. "It does look like it in the sun, Kathy. He wants a lock."

She couldn't help laughing. "Tell him, sorry. And that it's not gold."

Tony translated. Louis shook his kinky head and rattled off more Creole.

"He'd still like to have a piece, Kathy."

"Well, I'm afraid he can't."

"*Belle.*" Louis reached up to take hold of a lock between thumb and forefinger. He tugged gently. "Gimme?" he coaxed, looking up into her face.

"Louis, that's enough!" Scott spoke sharply. The boy's hand dropped to his side, and he stepped back from Kathy. He understood the tone, if not the words. "Do we play or don't we?" Scott appealed to Tony as interpreter.

"Sorry I interrupted," said Kathy. "Please go on with your game. I'll go talk to Claudine."

Claudine had kindled a charcoal fire outside the cottage and was brewing coffee. She had just finished cutting vegetables into a container made from half of a gourd and had a pot of water ready to go over the fire

63

in preparation for her family's evening meal. Kathy requested permission to photograph her and her husband. Fernand had gone to Furcy and would be along shortly, she was told. Meanwhile, she snapped the young woman as she poured coffee for the two of them.

During their chat, she learned that Claudine had had several years of schooling; that she and Fernand wanted more children but an infection had left him sterile; and that she liked Scott Blackburn. It pleased her that he permitted his son to play with hers. Also, he tipped generously for favors, like when she cooked Haitian meals for him. He especially liked her *calaloo*.

"And what is that?" Kathy wanted to know.

"Fine Creole soup," Claudine told her. "It made with crab, okra, tomatoes, onions. I season with thyme, bay leaf, and ground chili peppers. Is good. And I like to cook on big stove in kitchen."

Kathy had to smile at that. Whereas to Molly the old-fashioned wood stove was a gross inconvenience, to Claudine it was sheer luxury. She wondered what her reaction would be to the modern electric range.

On her way back to the house, Kathy saw that the horseshoe game had broken up. Fernand had returned and was talking to Scott, who beckoned her to join them.

"Fernand tells me there's been a death in Furcy. You game to go with me after dinner, Miss Miller?"

"Certainly, Mr. Blackburn." Even a death was grist for the writer's mill.

"Can I come too, Dad?" Tony piped up.

"No, you may not."

"But I went to Uncle Bill's funeral—why can't I go to this one?"

"They treat the dead differently here." A note of irritation had crept into Scott's voice. "I'm not sure myself what to expect."

"Aw, you'd think I was a baby. Why can't—"

"You heard me!"

Tony flushed and turned away without another word. It was the first time Kathy had heard his father speak to him harshly.

It was dark when they left for Furcy, and even before they arrived they could hear shouting and singing. Following the sounds Scott parked the Jeep near a yard lighted by tin lamps and torches. It was thronged with people. All the little neighborhood and beyond, apparently, had gathered there. Baskets of dried herring, biscuits, gingerbread, and a big pot simmering over hot coals indicated they were making a night of it. The women were bedecked in their Sunday best, including jewelry and their brightest kerchiefs. In one corner of the yard near a torch stuck in the fence, a group of men were playing cards; others were noisily shooting craps. Everybody seemed to be enjoying himself.

"This is a *wake*?" Kathy viewed the scene with astonishment.

"Try not to react in front of them," advised Scott as he helped her down from the Jeep. "Their idea of a wake is entirely different from ours."

People came crowding about them in welcome. *"Bonsoir, blancs."*

"The more the merrier," murmured Scott as they were escorted indoors to view the remains. The room was crowded. It seemed that all the chairs and stools and boxes in the neighborhood had been borrowed to accommodate visitors indoors and out. There was a table piled with more dried fish, gingerbread, and brown-sugar candy. Cups were being filled from a five-gallon jug of *clairin* and passed around. Family, relatives, and friends were sitting about eating, drinking, wailing, singing—having a great time, it seemed.

Kathy tried to keep herself from staring too intently. She noted that an old man with a kindly face had fallen asleep near the table. His head was leaning sideways, and someone had tied him to his chair with a sash so he wouldn't topple over. He wore blue cotton clothing and a straw hat on his woolly graying head. The noise around him didn't seem to disturb his slumber in the least.

One of the ladies urged Kathy toward the old man and seemed to want her to shake his hand. Gently, so as not to wake him, she took his hand in hers—and stiffened with shock as she realized *this was the corpse*.

With a gulp, she turned and stumbled toward Scott, who whispered, "Sorry. It dawned on me too late." He closed a warm hand about hers and kept her close beside him after that.

A youth politely offered the corpse a cup of rum and set it on the table before him. Then he asked Scott for a cigarette, lighted it and stuck it between the old man's lips. As the cigarette burned, the young man smiled and cried, "*Garder Papa fimer! Ça li fait plaisi'!*"

Scott spoke into Kathy's ear. "I think he said 'See Papa smoking. He seems to like it.' " His hand tightened around hers. "Your eyes are like saucers, Miss Miller. They mean no disrespect. They believe Papa's spirit is still hovering around and enjoying these little attentions. All this is to honor him. I know it seems shocking, and I've never seen anything like it myself, but really now—is the old boy grotesque just because he's propped up like that?"

Now that the initial shock had worn off, Kathy had to admit he seemed just a kindly old man, a little stiff in the joints, who had come to the party and fallen asleep.

"Do you want to take his picture?" Scott asked her, for she had brought her camera along. "It'd be a unique snapshot, to say the least."

"Would they mind?"

He spoke to the son, who relayed the request to his mother, the woman who had urged Kathy to greet the deceased. She assented, and Kathy snapped a picture of the old man sitting at the table with the cup of rum before him and the lighted cigarette in his mouth. Moving back, she took a second shot to include the family and relatives sitting around him. They regarded him with humorous affection, as though they thought he enjoyed having his picture taken.

All at once, there came a heartrending lamentation from the widow. It lasted a minute or two, then the wailer wiped her eyes and began chatting with the woman next to her as though nothing had happened.

Five minutes later, another grieving voice cried out with the same suddenness.

Scott leaned toward Kathy. "If there aren't enough lamentations during the death watch, it'll be held against the family; the deceased will be pitied for having been so little loved and respected by his kin. So they'll make sure the wailing continues on and off during the night—the louder, the better. When the family tires, relatives and friends will take over for them. I think we've seen enough."

On their way out, he gave the widow a couple of small bills to help defray funeral expenses. As they drove away, he said to Kathy, "You'll hear no voodoo drums tonight because of the death. And the burial has to take place before dawn. Otherwise, they believe, the deceased will shortly be followed by another member of his family. From what I could understand, it's to be a dancing funeral."

"Dancing funeral?"

"I saw one once. Two men carried the coffin on their heads, balancing it with their hands. They danced, zigzagging all the way to the grave, with the procession following behind, howling and making wild noises. The zigzagging and howling were to prevent evil spirits from entering the corpse." As Kathy remained silent, he added gently, "I know. It's bizarre. The Haitian peasants are difficult for the educated mind to understand. They hardly dare make a move without considering the effect on good and evil gods, *loas*. And because the spirits of the dead may become

67

loas themselves, great care is taken at funerals to release the dead properly. *Loas* are expected to provide for the faithful, and in turn must be served by them. I want you to record what we observed tonight. I may possibly do more than one book on Haiti, there's such a wealth of material here."

When they got home, Kathy headed straight for the typewriter to put down the details while fresh in her mind. Then she went to bed and tried to meditate on her children's story before going to sleep. It required considerable effort to banish the cigarette-smoking corpse from her mental screen; but, finally, another fragment of the story came to her and she bounded out of bed to capture it on paper. Would Tony enjoy the tale? she wondered. His reaction might prove helpful. Perhaps she should get his opinion before completing it.

In the morning, Kathy had private devotions in her room, and though it was only her first Sunday away from home, she found herself missing the little ones she taught in Sunday school. Her pastor's daughter was pinch-hitting for her until she got back. She hoped they would miss her.

She asked Tony for a little of his time before he went out to play, so as to get his opinion of *The Juggler*. She explained he represented the age group she was aiming for and, therefore, his reaction to her story might prove helpful.

"You mean you're a writer like my dad?"

"I'm a writer, yes." She said it firmly. "But I write for young people. Want to give me a little help?"

"What do I have to do?"

"Just listen to my idea and tell me what you think. Anything that comes to your mind. Let's go up to my room so we won't be interrupted. Or how about your room? I haven't seen it yet."

Tony's room adjoined his father's, with a private bathroom between. Like Kathy's, it faced the court-

68

yard, but had no private balcony. They made themselves comfortable on the plaid-covered bed.

"Now, Tony . . . my story is about a boy who loves to juggle things."

"A juggler? Hey, that sounds interesting."

"His name is Timmy, and he and his dad run a general store and gas station out West, off a desert highway. A lonely place, except for some scattered ranches—got that?"

"So?"

"So he's always juggling with the onions and potatoes in the store. But his father thinks he's wasting his time and wants him to quit fooling around and pay more attention to his work. I'm giving this to you briefly, Tony, because it isn't fully developed yet. Still, you can let me know if the idea holds your attention, okay?"

"Shoot. I like the juggling part. Is he gonna join a circus or something?"

Kathy smiled, pleased that she had captured his interest from the start. "Wait, Tony. What happens is that three bank robbers, who had killed a teller and gotten away with thousands of dollars, hide out at their place. And when the state troopers stop by, poor Timmy and his dad have to deny having seen the criminals because there's a gun trained on them from the back room."

"Didn't the troopers search the place?"

"No, because they really didn't believe the killers would come that way."

"Why not?"

"There's no place to turn off for fifty miles, and the police have set up a roadblock at the far end. The robbers would know that."

"Then how come—" Tony snapped his fingers, his face animated. "Oh, I get it! They *knew* the police wouldn't expect them to be there! And once the roadblock was lifted, they'd drive on through after dark and get away, huh?"

"You *are* bright."

"But they might kill Tim and his father first?"

"Right. Later, when the father is fixing sandwiches for the men at the snack bar, Timmy starts juggling potatoes. His dad tells him to cut it out, but Timmy says he might as well entertain the men while they're there. Anyway, because he's so quick and good at it, he's able to knock one guy out with a potato to the head, hit another on the nose, and even jostle the gun out of the killer's hand so that his father is able to grab it. Hmm . . . can you knock a man unconscious with a swift potato, I wonder? Anyway, it's Timmy's juggling ability that saves their lives and puts the criminals behind bars. A nice reverse ending might be the proud papa saying, 'You just keep right on practicing your juggling, son, hear? Anytime.' "

"Sounds good, Kathy."

"Think so? I'd better mull over that potato bit a little more. It bothers me."

Tony narrowed his eyes in thought. "Know what I'd do if I were Timmy? Learn to juggle the canned goods, too. A can is heavy and—"

"That's it!" Kathy leaned over and gave him an enthusiastic kiss on the cheek. "I don't know if you consider yourself too old for kisses, but—Tony, that's a *great* idea and I don't know why I didn't think of it. Thanks."

"Glad I could help." He grinned self-consciously, looking pleased with himself. "Do I get to read it when it's finished?"

"You sure do. By the way, do you know if your father has anything planned for today?"

"He's going to a cockfight. I've already been to one. Didn't like it."

"I think I'll go see if he'll take me along."

"Are you sure you want to go, Miss Miller?" was Scott's reply. "It'll be unpleasant, you know."

"It's not that I'm anxious to see birds fighting each other. But if it's part of Haitian life, I think I should.

70

I'm trying to observe all I can while I'm here. Isn't cockfighting a national passion of Haiti? Like baseball in America and bullfighting in Spain? I gathered that from your notes."

"True. There are fights every Saturday and Sunday at the stadium in Port-au-Prince, and many informal matches all over the island. I've been to one in the capital and I can't say I enjoyed it. I don't think you should go."

"Why are you going again if you didn't enjoy it?"

"I want to see one in the mountains for comparison. For me it's research in connection with my work."

"Well, it's research for me, too."

"Oh? For your writing?" He said it with a condescending smile that raised her ire. And when he suggested she let him read something of hers sometime, she thought, Not on your life! What was a simple little children's story to the world-renowned Scott Blackburn? No, thank you. Not that she couldn't take constructive criticism. But he might discourage her altogether, and she felt she couldn't risk it until she had gained more confidence in her ability.

Why was it they couldn't get along on an even keel? She wondered if he was like this with everyone or just with her. Every now and then he seemed to turn on her, for no real reason that she could determine. Oh, if only she could learn to just ignore his sarcasm and those flashes of patronizing rudeness and rejection. It wasn't easy.

The cockfights were about to start when they arrived. There was an excited crowd encircling the outdoor pit where the battles took place. Betting was frenzied, and *gourde* notes and *centime* pieces were passing from hand to hand. Before the combat began, each owner sucked the beak, neck, and spurs of his bird, and sniffed deeply under its wings. This, Kathy learned, was to show there was no poison used on them.

The cocks began by leaping at and over each other,

71

seeking to use their spurs in the classic manner. But they soon gave up these tactics to fight it out with their beaks.

The owners of the birds remained in the pit with them and seemed to go crazy. They gesticulated and crouched and leaped about—shouting, cursing, pleading, beating their breasts and the earth. The spectators also yelled and pleaded with the birds while blood and feathers flew.

Several times Kathy had to turn her head away; and when an eye was pecked out of the head of the losing fowl, she thought she was going to be sick. But her pride forced her to hold onto herself and see the thing through because she had insisted on coming. What a way to spend the Lord's Day!

The badly injured cock turned tail and ran, while the other, after pursuing him two or three times around the ring, stopped, strutted, and crowed shrilly in victory. The crowd went wild.

They left after three fights and two dead birds, and on the way home Kathy's revulsion burst loose. "Nauseating! Sadistic! How can a man raise an animal, tend it carefully day after day, only to destine it for a cruel, unnatural end? It's barbaric."

Scott pursed his lips thoughtfully. "I believe I can answer that. The average peasant's lot is a miserable one. He's poorer and hungrier today than he was fifty years ago. Their landholdings have shrunk, been divided and subdivided, and no longer feed them adequately. Fernand is well-off compared to some. You've seen the reddish tinge in the hair of some of the children?"

"What is that?"

"Malnutrition causes it. These people live on the edge of starvation much of the time. Not only that, they're plagued with diseases."

"Like what?"

"Malaria, syphilis, tuberculosis. Endless intestinal infections. It's a wonder the entire population doesn't go

72

berserk and destroy itself. Beneath that optimistic smiling exterior you can bet there's anxiety and frustration."

"What's all this got to do with cockfights?" Kathy wanted to know.

"Let me finish. They've got to have emotional outlets, you see. Doesn't everyone? For them, voodoo rituals are one. The cockfights are another—a release sadly lacking in sportsmanship, it's true. But are they any more barbaric than the bullfights in Spain, where the bull is tortured by a picador and teased by a torero before it's slain? You've never seen a bullfight, have you. I don't think you'd like it."

"Probably not. I can't stand to see animals abused. I had no idea the cockfights were so violent."

Scott shrugged. "You may not realize it, Miss Miller, but things like cockfights and voodoo help these people to survive. What else have they to look forward to?"

"But the cockfights are cruel, savage!" she protested. "How can you discuss it so calmly. I felt like screaming at those people. Poor birds."

"I warned you it wouldn't be pleasant," he reminded her.

"*That* was putting it mildly!"

He quirked an eyebrow at her. "Well, you needn't look at me as if I invented the game. It's brutal, I agree. But try to see it from the peasant's point of view. The only entertainment they have is what they can provide for themselves. They can't afford anything else. Yet for all the poverty and misery, crimes such as outright murder are rare in Haiti. Cockfights, you see, help to express aggressions. In that sense they serve a useful purpose."

"Maybe so. But they're wicked. Barbaric." As far as Kathy was concerned, no explanation could whitewash what she had witnessed today.

"What about boxing?" said Scott. "Is it not barbaric for human beings to batter each other to a pulp for money and recognition?"

73

It gave her something to ponder on the rest of the way home. But men *chose* to fight. Cocks were coerced into it. There was a difference.

Seeing she was still upset when he pulled the Jeep into the courtyard, he muttered, "I knew I shouldn't take you with me."

A little sob caught in her throat. "I keep seeing that poor cock . . . his eye ripped out of his head." She shuddered. "You should have told me what it'd be like."

"Come now, I gave you fair warning," he said sharply.

"Fair warning? You said it would be unpleasant. A mild word indeed for a cockfight. Gory, you should have said. A bloody mess, you could have said. Cruel, beastly, inhuman—*that's* what you should have said!" She was furious with herself for having gone, and aware that she was projecting self-anger onto him—but she couldn't seem to stop, though it was more his behavior pattern than her own.

The words seemed to echo in the silence that followed, harsh and unfair. But she had no desire to apologize. It felt good to strike out at him for a change.

She wasn't to have the last word. "After this, my dear Miss Miller, wait till you're *asked* to accompany me." He spoke with hauteur. "And now, be a good girl and go tend to your stories."

"Oh-h!" She glared at him and almost fell out of the Jeep in her haste to get away. The insolence of the man!

Chapter Six

The week went and Kathy settled routinely into her new way of life. Only once or twice did she permit herself to think wistfully of daily warm showers, the wonders of electricity, and the ice cream parlor back home, consoling herself with the thought that denial of the flesh strengthened character.

Boredom was no problem for her, and already she was ruminating on another story, about an American boy who took luxuries for granted until he got lost in Haiti and had to spend twenty-four hours among the peasants.

The Juggler was finished and Tony had approved the final draft, and she had put it away with a sense of satisfaction. To think she had more time to write here than at home—due to a wonderful part-time job that paid a generous full-time salary. She considered herself fortunate, despite the undercurrent of tension between her and her employer.

The novel—as yet untitled—was progressing nicely, and Scott did seem pleased with her work. With his permission, she wore slacks to the office and dressed up only for dinner.

And then it was the night of the voodoo ceremony being held near Furcy. Scott drove the Jeep as far as it was possible to go up a rutted trail, and parked. They were in the middle of the forest, it seemed, but they could see a light ahead and proceeded on foot, guided by the beam from Scott's flashlight. They could hear drums, and the closer they got, the more the sound enveloped them.

They broke through the narrow path into a large clearing. Before them was a compound of several huts and a *hounfor*, or voodoo temple, which was fronted by a peristyle, a thatched roof supported by hand-hewn posts and open on three sides. This was the area used for the voodoo dances and services. Near the entrance, a glowing-hot iron bar stood erect in a charcoal fire. In some of the nearby trees, skulls of animals hung from the branches.

Kerosene lanterns hung from the posts of the peristyle and cast flickering shadows on the beaten earth of the dance floor. People were standing in a loose semicircle some twenty feet back from the brightly painted central post. Although the drums were playing, the main ceremony had not begun, and friends and neighbors were chattering among themselves. Fernand and his family were there, and Scott greeted them and several other persons, who nodded and smiled and seemed not to mind his presence. His was a familiar face, and because Kathy was his guest she was accepted also.

There were chairs up front, and they sat in the second row. A moment later, a smiling man approached them. It was Pierre Rollet.

"*Bonsoir*, mademoiselle. How nice to run into you like this. And Mr. Blackburn, how are you?" He shook hands with them warmly and took the empty chair on Kathy's right. "I buy native handicrafts from these people," he told them, "and since they know me, I am permitted to attend a ceremony now and then. It is to be a *canzo*, I understand. I have seen this before, but no ceremony is exactly like any other, which is why I find them interesting."

"You speak Creole?" asked Kathy.

"Fluently. Perhaps I can interpret parts of the ceremony for you."

"We'd appreciate that," said Scott. He turned to

Kathy. "Mr. Rollet lives in Pétionville. I've been to his home, and he related some interesting material for my book."

"I am having a few friends over for dinner tomorrow night," Pierre told them. "It would give me great pleasure if you both would join us."

Kathy turned to Scott eagerly, her desire to go plain on her face.

"That's kind of you, Mr. Rollet," he said. "We'll be there."

"Cocktails at six. Dress comfortably, as you please."

"What is that iron bar in the fire?" Kathy asked him.

"That is the symbol of *canzo*. *Canzo* means 'to tie fire.' Mastery over fire, in other words. The red-hot bar is also a symbol of the *loa* Ogoun, or Ogu for short— god of the forge and of war."

Scott already had explained to her that the *canzo* was the second step an initiate must undertake to become a full-fledged voodoo member, and that it involved a trial by fire. There would be ritual dancing in which participants might become possessed by any one of the Haitian gods. The possessed one was "mounted" by the *loa*, and assumed the characteristics of the particular spirit who possessed him—meaning the god had entered into him. In this way the invisibles became visible. And because the *loas* were very much like the Haitian peasantry, sharing their tastes, habits, and passions, their behavior was not always what might be expected of supernatural beings. Indeed, they often spoke or behaved coarsely, swore, drank too much. Scott had warned Kathy to be prepared for whatever might occur, to take care not to betray any feelings of shock or disgust.

She looked about, making mental notes to be put down later on paper, since this was part of her job. Three men were sitting up front against the wall of the temple, beating drums of different sizes, the largest about five feet long. Near them was a makeshift altar covered with a white cloth, on which stood a pitcher, bowls, and other paraphernalia.

Now the *houngan* appeared out of the temple holding a pear-shaped gourd wrapped in strange-looking beads. Pierre explained they were snake vertebrae, in honor of Damballah. The gourd was a sacred rattle, the symbol of priestly office. Attached to it was a tiny bell to ward off evil influences.

Raising it in his right hand, the voodoo priest shook it vigorously toward the four cardinal points of the peristyle, as if in blessing. Then from the temporary altar, he picked up the pitcher and poured a little water at the base of the center post. Next, he took up a bowl, dipped his hand into it and took out a fistful of yellowish-white meal. Leaning over from the waist, he began drawing with it on the ground around the center post, letting the meal trickle in a steady stream between palm and little finger. As each handful was depleted, he reached into the bowl for more, working with astounding precision and never a rubout.

It was with amazement that Kathy watched intricate lacy patterns appear on the hard earth—until, finally, a beautiful mosaic of complex signs and designs had been completed, vivid as a chalk drawing on a blackboard. There were geometric forms, and birds and flowers, a heart, a snake twined about a sword. They were magical *vévé* drawings, symbols of the *loas* to be invoked tonight.

"That central post is very important in voodoo," said Pierre. "It is the ladder the gods use to come down and join their servants."

The priest placed his empty bowl on the altar, took up his sacred rattle and shook it. At once the drums modulated into a new, slower rhythm. Out the door of the temple glided his assistants, the *hounsi*—some eight or nine women dressed in white and wearing white scarves wrapped about their heads. A tall man led them. He was the *laplace*, the chief assistant, and he carried a sword against his shoulder. Two women

78

walked alongside him, bearing colorful sequined flags. Kathy wished she could have brought her camera, but Scott had advised against it.

As she sat observing the proceedings, a feeling crept over Kathy that she was being watched. Turning her head, she glanced over the faces behind her. They were all intent upon what was going on. Was she imagining things?

The drums changed beat as the procession marched around the central post and began to sing:

> *Atibô-Legba, l'uvri bayè pu mwê, agoé!*
> *Papa-Legba, l'uvri bayè pu mwê*
> *Pu mwê pasé.*

This part Scott was able to interpret for Kathy. They were asking Papa Legba to open the gate into the other world. He held the "key" and for this reason was identified with St. Peter. Legba was the go-between with the other *loas* for the people; therefore, he was saluted first of all *loas*.

As the *hounsi* danced around the central post, the delicate *vévé* drawings were erased by their shuffling bare feet. The drums increased their tempo, and a song to Ogoun followed. Some of the spectators leaped up to join the pantomime of praise.

Now a shift of mood with a change of rhythm— songs to Ezili Freda. Kathy recognized her name from Scott's notes. Ezili was the goddess of love and fertility.

The priest came forward. And all at once he seemed to go limp, his eyes closing. A murmur traveled around the crowd. It was unexpected, and even the *hounsi* seemed surprised. Two of them hastened to support him. A chair and a small table were brought out. They placed the priest in the chair, where he sat with his head hanging forward on his chest.

"Has he taken sick?" Kathy wondered aloud.

"He's in a trance," Pierre told her. "I think he has

been quietly mounted by the goddess Ezili. If so, he supposedly *is* Ezili. Watch."

While the drums continued to beat, the table was set with a bottle of wine, a empty glass, and a white plate of boiled meal, topped by a egg in its shell. Then two of the *hounsi* held a white sheet over the possessed priest, and he began to bend forward and back with great rapidity, toward the surface of the table and back to an upright position, his arms hanging quietly downward.

"What's he doing, Mr. Rollet?" asked Kathy.

"Ezili has accepted the food sacrifice. She is eating."

You've got to be kidding! thought Kathy.

The assistants were fluttering the covering sheet in such a way that she could not see the priest's upper torso. In less than a minute, his movements ceased. The sheet was removed. In the white dish only the broken shell of the egg remained. Some of the wine was gone from the upright bottle. The glass still had a little wine in it.

Kathy felt her jaw go slack. She could see a trickle of liquid egg yolk running from the corner of the priest's mouth—*yet not once had he lifted a hand to feed himself, nor had anyone reached in under the sheet.*

"Wow," murmured Kathy. She and Scott exchanged mystified glances.

"Good show," he commented.

Pierre chuckled. "You have not seen anything yet, my friends."

Wearily, the *houngan* rose and went into the inner sanctum, followed by his helpers, except for the *laplace*, who remained to set up an iron pot over the white-hot charcoals. Into this he poured a large jar of oil. As soon as it was hot, one of the women brought a bowl of what looked like dumplings from the altar and proceeded to drop them one by one into the sizzling oil. Sacred ritual food.

Meanwhile Kathy had the eerie sensation again of

eyes drilling into her head from somewhere behind her. She glanced over her right shoulder and then her left—and there at the side of the peristyle, among the standing onlookers, she saw familiar stony black eyes staring at her. *The mambo!*

It was like a shock wave washing over her, so that for a moment she felt almost paralyzed. Feeling her stiffen beside him, Scott gave her an inquiring glance. She turned her head to the front, murmuring something about so many strange faces, and made an effort to relax her tense body. She would not look behind her again, no. So what if the woman stared at her. She mustn't panic.

The earth trembled now under the muffled staccato of the drums, and Kathy felt sure her eardrums were turning black and blue. She could see the three drummers sweating profusely and marveled at their stamina.

Now two *hounsi* were leading a young girl draped in white out of the temple, the priest following. The other *hounsi* began to dance.

"The young girl is the *canzo* initiate for the trial by fire," Pierre explained. "She has been inside the temple several days in preparation for the *brulé zin*—the boiling pot."

Kathy sat on the edge of her chair as the initiate was guided to the iron pot over the white-hot charcoals. She saw that the priest was holding a bottle of rum. With a quick motion, he poured some of the liquor into the pot. Instantly, a blue flame shot high into the air. Someone screamed, and Kathy felt her heart give a jump. The drums crescendoed to a deafening level, the beat so frenzied she no longer could see the hands of the drummers. Tension mounted on all sides as the initiate was made to circle the pot.

She paused before it.

Abruptly, the priest seized her arm and plunged her hand into the boiling oil.

An awed murmur swept over the audience. Kathy gasped and hid her face against Pierre's shoulder. His arm encircled her waist comfortingly, and she was grateful for his support, feeling herself surrounded by supernatural forces which frightened her. Had she been alone, she might have leaped up from her chair and fled.

"Look up, mademoiselle, you do not want to miss this." Pierre's hand pressed her waist. "See, she is not hurt."

Kathy raised her head hesitantly and saw that the cult priest had lifted the girl's hand for all to see. It glistened with oil, but there was no sign of injury, nor did she flinch or make a sound. Again and again, the hand was dipped into the boiling oil. The last time, it emerged holding a brown ball of dough. The *houngan* smiled triumphantly, grabbed the dumpling and popped it into his mouth. Then the young girl was led back into the inner sanctum. Her trial by fire was over. She had graduated to *hounsi-canzo*, a full-fledged member of the voodoo society.

Kathy sighed and shook herself, feeling as though she were waking out of a trance. Incredible! Several explanations raced through her mind. Hypnosis. Or perhaps the skin was coated with a solution that made it impervious to heat. Or—was it done by the power of Satan? Whatever, it had been a spectacular performance.

No, I'm not going to look behind me again. Well . . . maybe just a glance.

Slowly and reluctantly, unable to resist the impulse, she turned her head over her shoulder.

The familiar face was gone. She let her glance roam over the crowd, but there was no sign of the *mambo*. Thank goodness she had gone. It was an uncomfortable feeling, knowing you were being watched by hostile eyes.

She saw Scott glancing at Pierre's arm that still encircled her waist. She had been about to disengage it, but now she changed her mind and let it remain. Impulsively, she moved closer to Pierre and whispered into his ear, something about the ceremony, knowing how it would appear to Scott. Let him know he wasn't the only fish in the sea.

The drummers were showing signs of exhaustion, and three men from the audience went forward to replace them. More people joined the dancers, including Fernand and his wife. Each person danced by himself as the whim took him, except when two came face to face; then they competed in agility and improvisation. The whole art of the dance, Kathy observed, seemed to be expressed less in the play of the feet than in the shoulder and hips.

Suddenly one of the dancers let out a shriek of alarm and surprise. It was Claudine. Her head jerked backward until her body was bent grotesquely like a drawn bow. It was as if a powerful invisible hand were tugging at her. Then, as though suddenly released, her upper torso swung violently forward, so that her head almost grazed the floor.

Kathy clasped her hands together nervously in her lap as she stared at her neighbor. Pierre's arm tightened about her waist. She turned to look at him, her eyes full of question marks.

"A spirit is attempting to take possession of her," he said.

Claudine was trembling all over and staggering wildly, her eyes like those of a terrified animal. Her husband followed her about to make sure she didn't hurt herself. It was no act, thought Kathy, watching the girl closely. She appeared to be struggling against the *loa*, fighting possession. The whole assembly was excited now, watching and waiting for the god to take over her mind and body.

Claudine reeled dizzily and collapsed on the ground. The *houngan* approached her and shook his gourd over her in time with the drums, calling out to her to let the *loa* enter their presence through her.

Slowly Fernand's wife lifted her head and got up from the ground. Assuming an arrogant masculine

83

stance with feet wide apart, and speaking in a loud male voice, she ripped out expletives one after the other—obviously violent oaths. No longer was her face that of a pretty young woman; it mirrored the rough, ferocious features of an angry male.

Good grief! thought Kathy, hardly able to believe her own eyes and ears. She could feel goosebumps rising on the back of her neck and along her arms. There was no question that it was a man's voice coming out of Claudine's mouth. At first she suspected ventriloquism, yet she could see the girl's throat muscles working as the voice spoke in cavernous tones.

"Ogu! Ogu!" someone cried out. It was the god of the forge and of war—the warrior god.

In haste the drums rolled a salute to the *loa*, who then demanded a bottle of rum from which he proceeded to drink heavily, emptying it halfway.

Ogu vanished as quickly as he had come, and Claudine resumed her normal expression and continued with her dance. It was as though a mask had been ripped off her face.

"She remembers nothing of what happened," Pierre explained. "If she did, she might be embarrassed by the language she used. But since it was Ogoun, she is not responsible. And you notice she is unaffected by all that rum?"

"Fantastic," breathed Kathy. Gently she disengaged his hand from her waist, and it seemed to her he withdrew it reluctantly, his fingers trailing caressingly across the small of her back. Out of the corner of her eye she saw Scott flick a downward glance, as though he'd been keeping tabs on the length of time the Frenchman kept his arm around her. The idea both pleased and irritated her. She wanted him to notice. Yet it was none of his business.

One thing, my dear Mr. Blackburn, you can be sure that if Pierre Rollet kissed me, he'd not then push me away.

The thought was oddly comforting and brought a faint smile to her lips.

It quickly vanished as among the dancers she saw a man seized by great undulating tremors that seemed to sweep from his feet upward to his head. His body arched itself strangely; then, suddenly, he threw himself to the ground and began to slither forward on his stomach, his tongue darting in and out as he crawled among the bare feet of the dancers.

It was too much for Kathy, and she closed her eyes.

Noting her distress, Scott said, "We can slip out now, if you like. There'll be more of the same, and then a feast that will last all night."

They said their good-byes to Pierre and left as inconspicuously as possible. They did not speak as they made their way back to the Jeep. Kathy felt exhausted, as though she herself had been dancing and knocking about all evening. She longed for the peace and quiet of her room.

Never would she forget this strange night. No, not if she lived to be as old as Methuselah.

Chapter Seven

Sunday afternoon Kathy washed her hair and had a shallow hot bath, a luxury up in the mountains. Since her blow dryer was useless without electricity, she brushed her hair dry while sitting in the sun on her balcony, and tea was sent up to her there.

She wondered what she should wear to Pierre's dinner party. Too bad she hadn't packed one of her long dresses. She selected a low-cut knitted black blouse with long, tight sleeves, and a flared black skirt. She dressed these up with a gold belt and gold jewelry. She braided her glossy hair and wound it atop her head in a coronet. Stepping into high-heeled patent leather pumps, she picked up her black clutch purse and white knitted cape, and gave her reflection a final appraisal. The blouse hugged her rounded breasts lovingly. The wide gold belt accentuated her slim waist. As for the braided coronet, it always made her feel as though she were wearing a crown, and this affected her bearing in a positive way. If one felt like a princess, one behaved like a princess. With her lips curved in a smile, she walked regally down the hall to the staircase.

Scott, fortunately, happened to be going up the stairs at the same time Kathy started down. Whether the princess was holding her head too high to watch her footing or was daydreaming, she miscalculated her step and found herself suddenly pitching forward into space, her hold torn from the banister. Purse and cape went flying as she threw out both hands in an effort to save herself.

In a swift blur of movement, Scott leaped diagonally up the stairs to break her fall. As she slammed against him, one arm clamped about her, while with the other hand he caught at the banister to steady himself. Then both his arms were holding her safe; and she clung to him with fluttering breath, pressing her face into his broad shoulder. She tried to control her trembling, taking comfort in his strength. Oh, if he hadn't been there! She shuddered to think what might have happened.

Lifting her head, she saw he had gone white beneath his tan. Her peril had shaken him badly. His face was so close to hers she could see her own minuscule reflections in his pupils. His eyes were arresting this close, and as she looked into them it was the same as that night in the study—she could not seem to avert her gaze. She had not known, before meeting this man, that it was possible to be aware of another person to the very core of her being.

She heard him catch his breath, felt his chest lift against hers, and sensed a conflict raging within him. Before she could step out of his arms, they became steel bands imprisoning her, and his mouth claimed hers, sending a wild thrill all through her body to her very bones.

No! This time, though her flesh yearned toward him as before, she would not respond, she would *not*. He wasn't going to have another opportunity to reject her, not if she could help it. She tried to struggle, but her efforts were futile within his steel embrace.

When his head lifted, her lips felt bruised and burning. He released her abruptly. "Sorry, Miss Miller. I-I don't know what came over me," he muttered.

Miss Miller. Even after two intimate kisses. She did not know whether she felt like laughing or crying. But she did know she was glad she hadn't responded to his kiss, hadn't let him make a fool of her a second time.

She saw that his face looked strained, distressed. He ran restless fingers through his hair and shuffled his feet; this time it was he who felt embarrassed and constrained to offer an explanation, for in a low voice he said, "In the year since I lost my wife . . . I've not touched a woman. I suppose that's why—look, I apologize. You're attractive . . . and I'm not exactly made of stone. But it won't happen again."

"I should hope not—not if it's so painful for you," she said coldly. It was with grim satisfaction that she watched warm color stain his cheeks. "Anyway, thank you for saving me from a bad fall. Are we leaving soon?"

"I'm on my way up to change." He gathered up her cape and purse and handed them to her, not quite meeting her eyes.

"I'll be with Molly when you're ready." She brushed past him, taking care where she placed her feet.

Molly's bright blue eyes made no attempt to conceal anything.

"You saw?" said Kathy.

The gray head nodded. "I was near the doorway. Thank God he caught you. You could be at the bottom of the stairs right now with a broken neck."

"I know." Kathy shivered and sank into a chair. "Can you spare a few minutes?"

Molly closed the door before joining her at the table. "That kiss—not the first time? But who can blame him. A pretty lass like you."

"That's all I am to him—just another pretty girl," said Kathy dejectedly.

Molly laid a hand over hers. "You like him, Kathy, eh? More than a little, I'll wager."

Molly was a shrewd one who missed little of what went on around her, Kathy realized. And she had a feeling you couldn't fool her. Either you told her the truth or kept your mouth shut. And since there was no one else to confide in or to advise her, she decided to speak frankly.

"He doesn't want me falling in love with him, Molly. And it bothered him that he kissed me. Yet we're both unattached, and it's not as though he lost his wife just recently. Why shouldn't he kiss a girl? Why shouldn't he fall in love again? I don't understand why he fights it so. The first time—yes, you guessed right, he did kiss me once before. And then seemed terribly angry and upset over it. What is it? Is he still in love with his wife?" And as Molly shook her head to that Kathy continued, "Then it's something about me he objects to. He finds me attractive—he said so. Yet I rub him the wrong way. He gets impatient with me over nothing. Sometimes he's so *rude*. I've never affected anyone that way before."

" 'Tain't you, child." Molly gave her hand a sympathetic squeeze. "Glad I am you can talk to me, what with your own mother so far away. I'm a widow, Kathy, and I raised two daughters and a son—so no need to be bashful with me. I don't have much education, but life itself is a great teacher, and I got an instinct about people, you know? Now listen to me, dearie. The boss been barking at everybody, not just at you. That goes for Tony and me. With me you should hear him sometime. This man, he's not been himself since the wife died. Before that, he seldom lost his temper, was never mean. Now he's having tight nerves and trouble sleeping."

"Then you don't think it's me personally that irritates him?"

Molly shook her head. "The least thing can set him off."

She let out a sigh. "I always know when he's had a bad night. Not even do I have to see him to know."

"How's that?"

"Usually he's neat as a paper of pins. When he's restless at night he leaves a trail of his books and papers behind him in the study. 'Tis a sure sign. That be how I know to bring coffee upstairs. Thank goodness it helps, along with aspirins, so he can get on with his work. But the guilt—that's wearing him down, poor man."

"Guilt?" Kathy straightened in her seat. "What guilt?"

"That sad night—" Molly broke off and placed a warning finger against her lips. "I think he be coming," she whispered. "Quick change, that. We talk another time."

Scott stuck his head in the doorway. "Ready," he said.

He had changed to a gray leisure suit. With it he wore a paisley print shirt in cool greens and blues. No matter what he had on, he always looked the virile male, thought Kathy as she joined him. Beautifully proportioned, he moved with the lithe, fluid grace of a tiger.

She wondered what Molly had meant by a "guilt" complex. Was he somehow responsible for his wife's death?

They were quiet on the way to Pétionville, and she knew they both were thinking of the incident on the stairs. His apology rankled, nor did she understand it. From now on, she must keep tight rein on her emotions. Theirs was a business arrangement, and she must not allow herself to forget that. The social engagement tonight—it wasn't a real date and meant nothing.

The Rollet residence was set among palm trees, and their host greeted them warmly by their first names. "After all, we are friends, are we not? Please call me Pierre. Ah, Kathy"—his lips brushed her hand—"you look charming, my dear. Black does something for that lovely hair of yours."

She smiled and thanked him. He had a gift for making a woman aware of her femininity, and she suspected he took advantage of it whenever the opportunity presented itself. She wondered if there could be a Madame Rollet, though she was inclined to doubt it.

He introduced them to his other guests: a middle-aged French couple, a good-looking mulatto gentleman and his bronze fiancée, and a fragile doll of a Chinese-Haitian with lustrous tilted eyes—Pierre's date. He then brought up the topic that had been in Kathy's mind, as though he had read her thoughts.

"I find the bachelor life most conducive to meeting such lovelies as Lotus here," he said, slipping an arm about the girl's tiny waist. And with a roguish twinkle in his eye, "Is it not fortunate that many young ladies, rather than just one wife, have the privilege of my company? Indeed, I hope to keep it that way." He joined in the laughter, though he obviously was not joking. "Now, Kathy, what would you like to drink? Scott? I can mix anything."

Since she did not drink much, she requested he fix something light and sweet for her. Scott suggested a daiquiri, light on the rum, and a dry martini for himself.

The men were attired in casual wear. The women wore gowns. Again Kathy regretted not having brought one from home. She loved long dresses and the fact that nowadays they came in styles suitable for both formal and informal wear.

As they sat by the fire with drinks in hand, conversing over soft music from the stereo, she took in her surroundings. The rug was salmon and gold, as were the patterned draperies, and there were touches of bronze and green about the room. The furniture was French, elegant. Through an archway she could see a beautifully set dining table, with a crystal chandelier overhead. French doors opened from the living room onto a screened patio containing wicker furniture and tubs of live greenery. It was a lovely house, undoubtedly run by a housekeeper. From the look of things, Pierre's business was a prosperous one.

Kathy made her daiquiri last, and did more listening than talking. The conversation that flowed about her touched on France and England and the United States, then settled on Haitian politics, of which she knew little. The power behind the throne, the mulatto gentleman insisted, was the president's sister more so than Claude "Baby Doc" Duvalier himself. As for the secret

91

police, though they no longer were so obtrusive as to frighten away the tourists, they were still about, never doubt.

Kathy absorbed everything like a sponge. She noticed the almond-shaped eyes of the Chinese beauty followed Pierre's every move and gesture, and she found herself hoping the girl wasn't in love with him. There probably was a mile-long trail of broken hearts behind the handsome Frenchman, and this girl would not be the last on his string. One thing could be said for him, however—he made it clear that marriage was not in his plans for the future. At least he was honest about it so that his women knew where they stood.

The dinner was served by a Haitian maid hired for the occasion and included *tasso*, strips of beef "cooked" in lime juice for hours in the sun—Pierre explained this to Kathy—and Creole lobster. For dessert there were miniature pastries, and chocolates that had nuggets of ice cream as their centers. A most delicious meal.

It was late by the time the party broke up and everyone said their good-byes. Scott and Kathy were the last to leave, except for the almond-eyed Lotus. Kathy suspected she was staying the night.

As her host escorted her to the door, she told him how much she had enjoyed the evening.

"Ah, but you must come again," he said softly, and from the way he smiled into her eyes and from the intimate pressure of his hand upon hers, she knew he meant alone. Though at the moment he had the Chinese-Haitian under his spell, he already was looking forward to his next conquest.

It won't be me, Pierre. But you do have a way about you, I must admit.

Kathy had spoken little to Scott all evening, and on he way home in the Jeep she gathered aloofness about her like a protective cloak. They had almost arrived when, glancing at her sideways, he said, "That Frenchman seems to have his eye on you."

He had noticed. Well, good for him.

"I like him." She said it deliberately, and saw him frown.

"He's a philanderer. I hope you realize that."

"But a charming philanderer, don't you think?" she said perversely.

His lips tightened. They had reached the house, and he drove around back and braked so abruptly, she jerked forward in her seat. She caught the glint of his eyes and knew he was angry, though why he should be escaped her.

Facing her, he said curtly, "Look, Miss Miller, you're alone here in a strange country. I can't help but feel responsible for you."

"Oh, is that it?" she said, her chin going up. "Well, I'm of age and my private life isn't any of your concern, thank you all the same."

"I'm afraid I have to disagree, especially now that a man like Rollet has taken an interest in you. I like the fellow well enough, but there's only one thing on his mind when it comes to women. Stay away from him."

"Is that an order?"

"A warning."

"I don't need your warning. I'm not stupid." And she added defiantly, "But I'll see him if I want to."

"You little fool!" His lean fingers reached over to grip her arm as though he wanted to shake her. "Like it or not, I'm going to look after you. Is that understood?"

"No, it is *not* understood!" she flared, her temper ignited by his overbearance. She twisted out of his grasp. "How dare you dictate what I should and shouldn't do!" Impotent tears sprang to her eyes. "Oh, I-I think I hate you!"

She attempted to get out of the Jeep, but he pulled her toward him and this time he did shake her. "Listen to me, little lady! I hadn't intended telling you this. I phoned my sister a couple days ago and your mother was there. Apparently they're good friends, and Lucy

93

is leaving for Canada tomorrow. She—your mother, that is—got on the phone and requested that I look after you. It's the first time you've been away from home, eh? Well, it seems I'm obligated to keep an eye on you whether I want to or not." He let her go. "Now you understand?"

Kathy groaned and put up her hands to her face. "How *could* she!" The final humiliation. As though she needed a guardian. "You can't take Mother's request literally." Her eyes shot sparks at him. "I won't have it, do you hear? I'm not a child!"

"Then stop behaving like one," he retorted. "Now stay put for a minute." He got out of the Jeep to open the garage doors, then climbed back in and drove forward to park inside. Cutting off the motor, he turned on a flashlight and went around to help Kathy down. But she brushed aside his extended hand and hopped out in a fury, whereby she promptly fell to her knees. Gripping her arm, he lifted her to her feet and half led, half pulled her across the yard and into the house, all without a word, making her feel like a chastised brat.

If he thought he was going to direct her private life, he had another think coming, she fumed inwardly. As for her mother, she'd have plenty to say to her when she returned home.

His beam cut a path up the main staircase and down the narrow left hall to her room. He waited while she lit her lamp, looking grim and determined, and then silently left her.

Tears of fury and frustration coursed down her cheeks as she pulled off her clothes, threw on a pair of pajamas and flopped into bed. Oh, that man! How could she possibly be attracted to him? Right now she could gladly wring his neck.

Chapter Eight

For the next couple of days, tension ran high between Kathy and Scott, and she spoke to him only when spoken to. But one couldn't remain uptight indefinitely, and when she found herself making an unusual number of errors in her work, she knew she had to come off her high horse, if only for the sake of the novel. A salary like hers obligated her to do her finest work, as did her pride. And so she mentally forgave him his highhandedness, though it wasn't easy, and went on from there. At least she no longer felt like wringing his neck.

Then one wonderful day he approached her on the patio where she lay reading while awaiting tea, and handed her an envelope forwarded from home. Seeing the name *Cricket* on the left-hand corner, she jerked upright on the chaise longue, excitement stabbing through her. *Cricket* was a top juvenile magazine to which she had submitted one of her stories.

"Something good?" Scott had noticed her reaction.

She hesitated only a moment, then tore open the envelope. It was a check. She stared at it incredulously. "Two hundred dollars!" she gasped. "I can't believe it!"

"A nice round sum," he observed. "Somebody likes you, eh?"

"It's from an editor." She said it proudly. "And this is my second sale."

"Well, congratulations." He looked surprised. "I had no idea the juvenile markets pay that well."

"Most of them don't." She drew in a deep breath

and expelled it gustily. "Oh, I'm so happy!" she exclaimed with youthful exuberance.

He smiled understandingly. "So you really *do* work at your writing," he murmured. "It appears I owe you an aplogy. It's getting to be a habit with me, isn't it? Would you be willing to let me read something you've written? Bring any manuscripts with you?"

"I wrote a new story here. Believe it or not, your son gave me some help on it. I'll go get it," she said, rising. Now she could afford to let him criticize her work. Even if he tore it apart, she could take it. This check in her hand had given her new confidence. It was proof of her talent and had come from a fine magazine. At this moment she knew without a shadow of a doubt that she was a writer, a professional writer, no matter what Scott Blackburn thought of her work.

Braced for negative comments, she was elated when his judgment of her story turned out favorable. He felt it had a message, and he liked her style. As for his criticisms, they were minor—a phrase or two that could be improved upon.

"You built up the suspense in such a way it wasn't obvious the juggling would become a weapon. Very good. Though I've read only this one story, it's plain you can write. And I'm sure it takes a very special talent and a love for children to be able to write for them. Don't let anything discourage you, Kathy."

Kathy. Several times now that name had slipped from his lips, and it seemed to have a special sound when he pronounced it. Did he think of her as Kathy, though he called her Miss Miller? And he *liked* her story. It made her choke up with happiness.

The days passed pleasantly for her. Many were the solitary walks she took, in which her soul rejoiced at the magnificent panorama of Haitian mountains and valleys. At such times she felt overwhelming gratitude for the opportunity to view the beauty in this part of the world. Surely this job was a gift from above.

She learned to toss horseshoes so as to make an occasional ringer, and she played checkers with Tony, who won two games out of three. She even picked up a few words in Creole, which she proudly displayed in a letter home. She swam and sunbathed with Tony at the pool, and her skin darkened while her hair lightened. Not being one of those delicate blondes who burns and peels, she acquired—with the help of tanning lotion—a rich golden skin tone that made the color of her hair stand out all the more. The mountain air and exercise, the good food and simple life agreed with her. She felt marvelous.

One day they all went on a picnic, even Molly, and the food tasted extra good in that beautiful waterfall setting. They played ball, swam, sunbathed—a wonderful day, and Kathy took pictures. Only once did Scott flare up. That was when Tony stumbled over him as he lay with eyes closed on his towel. He sat bolt upright and slapped the child on his thigh hard enough to bring tears to his eyes.

At once he pulled Tony down beside him and held him close in the curve of his arm as he said contritely, "I'm sorry, son. Want to swat me back?"

"Aw, Dad . . ." Tony rubbed his thigh and said ruefully, "Hey, man, your muscles wouldn't even feel my hand, and you know it."

"How about playing catch, just you and me." His father was anxious to make amends, and Tony softened.

The women watched them move away from the pool, and Molly said, "What did I tell you, Kathy? Never he used to flare up like that for such a little thing."

"Molly, before they come back—you mentioned something about guilt, remember?"

Memories darkened the older woman's eyes as she said, "She was killed by a drunken driver, you know. His wife Joan. A lovely woman, blond and trim, with blue eyes. But him it was"—inclining her head in Scott's direction— "that insisted she go out with him that night to the cinema. She didn't feel like going, but he wanted to see the picture and wanted her with him. And that was the end for her, poor thing, God rest her soul."

"How sad," murmured Kathy. No wonder he felt responsible.

"Happened at an intersection," Molly went on in a husky voice. "Scott was driving. The other vehicle, it slammed into her side of the car, killing her and the baby she was carrying. Him, just a broken collarbone. It's been torturing his mind all these long months, I can tell. And one night back home, just before we came here, I heard him cry out: 'Oh, Joan, it should have been me, *me*!' Is that guilt or no? He can't forgive himself, nor will he talk about it. I tell you, Kathy, it would help him if he could talk about it to somebody."

For a moment they were silent as they watched the two play ball. Scott and Tony wore identical navy-blue trunks and were beautifully bronzed by the sun, Tony a shade darker than his father.

"A fine figure of a man," said Molly. "And a good husband too. He had control of his temper in those days and was a reasonable man. You know what he used to say? That when you're right, you can afford to keep your temper; when you're wrong, you can't afford to lose it." And with a shrewd glance at Kathy, "What he's needing is to love again. Some nice young woman he can open up to and pour out the hurt what's inside him. Then the wound can heal. I wonder . . . maybe hearts aren't finished till they be broken. Like buds that have to burst before they're perfected." A sigh escaped her. "Someone who cared could do more for that man than any psychiatrist—I'd be willing to wager a year's salary on it. Kathy, child, when you came— well, I was hoping you would be the one."

"Molly, I'm glad you like me, and I do like you. Very much. But I told you, he doesn't want to become romantically involved."

"Poppycock!" Molly made a gesture of dismissal. "He's a normal male with normal desires. He kissed you, didn't he? 'Tis the guilt what keeps him from following through. He's punishing Scott Blackburn for his wife's death, whether he realizes it or not—by denying himself another chance at love and happiness. That's how I see it, Kathy."

Kathy stared into the kindly face. It sounded so plausible. "Why, Mrs. Maguire, I do believe you're an amateur psychologist."

"Maybe so. Like I say, life itself teaches one. Listen, lassie, I been thinking. Could be he's extra rough on you on account of fighting the attraction he feels for you."

"Oh? So what do I do now?"

Molly cocked an eyebrow at her. "I know what *I'd* do if I were you. Set my cap for him and keep sweet—yes, even when he's nasty. You know, Kathy, a smile is a curve that can set a lot of things straight. Stay sweet, and the time is coming when he'll break down and let himself love you. He's built a fence round his heart, but how long can he go on like this? After all, a healthy young man . . . and without a wife for so long. That makes him vul—what's that word?"

"Vulnerable? Sure, vulnerable to *any* woman. Which means the attraction he feels for me is purely biological, doesn't mean a thing."

"Ah, but Kathy, it gives you a weapon, don't you see? You could *make* it mean something. Before some other woman does—and soon there *will* be another woman here, a very beautiful one. I tell you, he's the best. Or was—and can be again."

"You're suggesting I chase after him?" Kathy's tone expressed indignation.

Molly laid a hand over hers, the corners of her lips twitching. "Come now, lass, women been chasing men all through the ages, one way or another. In this case, it's necessary. Because of his guilt feelings." She paused and frowned. "What worries me is that the

99

wrong kind might go after him. Be bound to happen sooner or later. And the boy, he's needing some-body who'll love him as well as his father. Somebody—well, like you." She heaved a gusty sigh. "I've been praying about it."

Kathy looked at her suspiciously. "You wouldn't be trying to make me feel responsible, Molly? I've never chased a man in my life. I do have some pride, after all."

Molly heaved yet another sigh but refrained from saying anything more. The sigh said it all and seemed to linger on in Kathy's mind.

Scott and Tony were doing pushups now, and Kathy could tell the boy had forgot all about the slap. Despite occasional flare-ups, he knew his father loved him.

They rejoined the women, and Scott threw himself down on his towel laughing—a rare and wonderful sound, thought Kathy. It made her feel good to hear it, and she wished he could laugh like that more often. Perhaps a new love *could* help him pull himself to-gether, she found herself thinking wistfully. But for her deliberately to entice him—she just couldn't be that calculating. And even if she made the attempt, she doubted she could pull it off. She lacked sophistication. She blushed too easily. He'd see through her in a minute, and that would be too humiliating.

Two days later, in one of his dark moods, Scott lit into her as though spoiling for a fight.

"Miss Miller," he said sternly, "why did you change one of my phrases in that last chapter we did?"

She gave him a blank stare. "What phrase? I wouldn't presume to change anything."

Picking up her typed copy, he read aloud, emphasiz-ing the offensive phrase, " '. . . giving him a *wide, white smile*, the politician assured him he wished him a pleasant stay in Hiati.' What I dictated, my dear Miss

Miller, was *travel-poster smile*. I'll thank you to leave the revisions to me," he concluded harshly.

Kathy counted to ten while she checked back on her shorthand notes, knowing exactly what she'd find. "I'm sorry, Mr. Blackburn, but you did say 'wide, white smile.' It's right here in my notes."

"I distinctly remember having the other phrase in mind," he persisted, scowling at her.

"Perhaps you had it in mind, but it's not what you dictated." There was an edge to Kathy's voice. "Since 'travel-poster smile' is obviously the more descriptive phrase, why on earth would I substitute the other?" she reasoned.

"Why indeed!" Apparently he could not concede he might be mistaken; it would necessitate another apology, his fourth, and he was not about to give it.

Kathy stood her ground. Be sweet no matter how he behaved? Molly was asking a lot. He was utterly impossible at times.

"Even authors make mistakes," she couldn't resist adding as a parting shot.

"*And* secretaries," he said icily, having the last word. "See that you make the correction."

By lunchtime, he had got hold of himself. After clearing his throat self-consciously, he asked Kathy if she'd like being shown something of the highlights of Port-au-Prince. They could take Tony along and have dinner in the city. Realizing it was his way of making amends, and because she did want to see the capital, she said she'd love to go. Tony, of course, was all for it.

On their way down the mountain, they stopped at the castlelike Jane Barbancourt rum factory. There, on a terrace overlooking a jungle below, they tasted— courtesy of the house—delicious rum liqueurs, including banana, mango, hibiscus, and coffee-rum. Scott purchased fifths of several flavors.

In Port-au-Prince, they visited the Roman Catholic cathedral with its magnificent stained-glass windows, and the Episcopal cathedral, where Kathy was entranced by the primitive murals done by Haitian artists. She found it whimsical that at *The Last Supper* all the attendants at the feast were portrayed as Haitian—except for Judas, who was a white man.

Everywhere they went, ragged people came rushing toward them to offer, urge, almost force upon them garish paintings, straw hats, scuffies in raffia. Vendors stood outside hotels, restaurants, and shops, and they were forever converging on likely prospects.

After Kathy viewed and was properly impressed by the spacious Champ de Mars with its lawns, drill grounds, monuments, and imposing government buildings, Scott took her to the huge Iron Market, so named for the use of iron in its construction. A sort of farmer's market, it took up two blocks and teemed with Haitians bartering, bargaining, selling everything from watches to sculptures, nuts to notions. A bubbling cauldron of humanity, Kathy found the place hard to take, for the poverty was heartbreaking; and the heat, the noise and the crowds were exhausting. Though you could buy some great bargains here, there were too many distractions, and already she felt tired.

Goats, donkeys, and half-naked urchins abounded in the streets, and some of the children ran after the Jeep begging for money. When she tossed them some coins, they thanked her with happy grins, and one little fellow waved until the Jeep turned a corner out of his sight. Kathy couldn't help but marvel that these people could smile at all. Their vitality and *joie de vivre* was astonishing in the face of the poverty that surrounded them.

Port-au-Prince, she decided, was not just a city, it was a whole experience—it was sights and sounds and smells such as one seldom encountered. The contrasts were incredible, and ranged from grand modern structures to Victorian gingerbread houses to small wooden hovels; from incessant taxi horns and human voices to the braying of donkeys and the barking of dogs; from exquisite flower fragrances to the stink of rotting garbage. A blend of the old and the new and the bizarre, the capital was just too much. Overwhelmed, Kathy found herself longing for quieter surroundings and was grateful when Scott suggested they find a place to eat.

"About time," said Tony, and his stomach agreed by emitting a loud growl.

They dined at La Sélect on the road to Pétionville, where authentic Haitian dishes were served in an informal atmosphere. Here Kathy's nerves quieted down and she was able to relax and enjoy her food. Having missed tea, the three of them were ravenous and did full justice to the meal.

Home again, and having thanked Scott for an interesting and colorful day, Kathy retired to her room and went straight to bed.

That night, she saw herself dressed in bridal white going up the church aisle at home on her father's arm. And then he drew back her veil and kissed her, and turned her over to the bridegroom—Scott! Their eyes met, and his smile was so full of love and tenderness, her heart quivered with bliss—and she found herself sitting upright in bed with both hands clasped to her breast, filled with a joy such as she'd never known.

A dream! Just a dream. But why such a one? Did she love this man?

I don't know, I'm not sure. He keeps a wall between us.

She sat there on the bed, hugging herself, feeling yet the thrill of looking into the bridegroom's face and finding it was Scott. For any girl to marry such a man would be to take a giant step upward in the world—a famous name, wealth, everything. And a dear young boy named Tony. What more could a woman ask for?

Was it possible Scott Blackburn could love her? Suppose she did make herself irresistible to him—it would mean calculating her every look and gesture to keep him aware of her as a desirable woman. Oh, but the risk of making a fool of herself was great.

She couldn't do it. But perhaps before the summer

was over, he would resolve his inner conflict and look upon her with a new attitude. Then they could really get to know each other and fall in love openly and naturally.

It was a pleasing thought. She lay back on her pillow smiling to herself as she fantasized him being sweet and attentive, kissing her out of love rather than because he was driven to it by his libido.

She *could* love him—easily. But he'd have to take down that fence around his heart and let her in. She would not stoop to cajoling her way in just because he was vulnerable. She did not want him just to want her. She wanted him to love her.

Her thoughts turned to Olivia Borelli. She was to arrive on Monday. Scott had said she was beautiful. Molly had said "very beautiful." How beautiful could she be, Kathy wondered, feeling an odd stab in the region of her heart.

Chapter Nine

On Monday afternoon Scott and Tony drove to the airport to pick up their guest, and took along letters to
mail for Kathy. Shortly after the Jeep had departed,
she went for a walk and ended up at the pool, her favorite spot. Tony's friends were there, splashing about
in the nude, while their mother washed clothes at the
edge of the stream into which the pool overflowed. The
boys shouted and waved at the sight of Kathy, without
any self-consciousness concerning their state of
undress, and she returned their greeting and went to sit
near Claudine on a slab of rock.

"It's quite a climb up here. How do you do it in
bare feet, Claudine? Don't the stones hurt you?"

"My feet like leather," Claudine told her humorously. "Stones not bother me." She was on her knees,
leaning over a wide flat rock on which she was lather-
ing one of her husband's shirts with a bar of brown
kitchen soap. Looking at her pretty features and slim
form, it seemed incredible to Kathy that this young
woman had acted out the role of a bold and vulgar *loa,*
using vile language and consuming half a bottle of raw
rum. Had someone described it to Kathy, she would
not have believed it of Claudine. But her own eyes and
ears had witnessed the phenomenon; she herself had
seen the girl's face undergo a startling change, had
heard her rip out what were obviously curse words in a
rough male voice.

Pierre had said the possessed remembered nothing

once they were "mounted" by a *loa*. She wondered if that were true.

Cautiously she said, "Claudine, that *canzo* ceremony a couple weeks ago? I found it most interesting. But when you became Ogoun, well, it scared me. And when you drank half a bottle of rum, I thought for sure you'd be staggering after that. But it didn't seem to affect you."

The brown hands paused in their work as Claudine turned to look at her frowningly. "Half a bottle, you say? That much?"

"That much. And straight down almost without a pause."

Claudine gnawed on her lower lip. "Fernand not tell me," she murmured. "Only that Ogu mount me."

"And you don't remember?"

She shook her head.

"You don't recall shouting and using rough language?"

"I do that?" Claudine turned her face away with an embarrassed little laugh. "Was not me," she mumbled, attacking the shirt with vigor. *"Loa Ogu,* he say whatever he want to say. Me, I not use bad language. And I cannot drink half a bottle *clairin* all at one time. Make me sick. It was the *loa,* mam'selle. He mount me and make me his horse."

"I see." Kathy could not doubt the girl's sincerity. It was possible that some pretended to be mounted by *loas*. But she felt Claudine was telling the truth. Of course, she had her own ideas as to who and what these *loas* were.

Kathy sat watching Claudine as she worked over the shirt, using the rock as a washboard. Dipping the piece in and out of the stream to rinse off the suds, she twisted it firmly several times between her hands and spread it on a sun-kissed bush while she finished the rest of her wash.

"Where's Fernand? I haven't seen him around today?"

106

"He gone since early." Claudine soaped up a small pair of jeans. "To visit sons. Be back tomorrow. Or maybe next day."

Kathy gaped at her stupidly after glancing toward Marc and Louis. Noting her puzzlement, Claudine sat back on her heels and explained patiently, "Fernand have four sons before infection ruin his seed. Two by me—two by *placée.*"

"*Placée?* I don't understand."

"Number Two wife."

"Oh?" Was polygamy practiced on this island? "You don't mind, Claudine?"

"Why I should mind?" Claudine bent over the rock to continue her work while they talked. "When Fernand marry me, he already have two properties and need *placée* to take care of another one. Is one hour walk from here. There he build other *caille,* another garden, and make second family to take care of it. He go see them every week. But I his first wife," she added proudly.

Amazing, thought Kathy. Not even a hint of jealousy. Perhaps because the two families lived apart. Was it standard procedure in this country? She made a mental note to look it up when she returned to the house.

After Claudine had finished her wash, she began stripping to bathe, and at this point Kathy left her and walked back to the house.

In the study, she went through Scott's notes until she found a card marked PLACÉE. Reading through it, she discovered the arrangement known as *plaçage* had complete community sanction. A man whose energies and good fortune made an extra household possible was expected to make such an arrangement. The woman who occupied the second and even the third household was not considered a concubine, but a wife. Like the first wife, she had prestige in her community, and authority and responsibility. Her position and her rewards were similar to those of the first wife, though

107

her marriage was not consecrated by a church or civil ceremony—but, then, neither was that of many first wives.

Kathy put away the card. It was difficult to imagine such an arrangement without the element of jealousy being present. Most women would not tolerate such a situation. But, apparently, in Haiti it was the accepted mode of life among the peasants.

She went to the kitchen to visit with Molly, who was sitting in a rocker knitting a small red sweater. "Let's have tea together in here," Kathy suggested, pulling up a chair for herself. "The others won't be back in time. I guess Mr. Blackburn told you, huh? They'll be having tea in the city before starting back. Who are you knitting for?"

"My youngest granddaughter. Seven years old. Loves the color red."

"How many grandchildren?"

"Eight. The oldest granddaughter is getting married in September." Molly smiled. "Could be I become a great-grandma before I leave this world, eh? Who you got in your family, Kathy?"

"My mother, two brothers, and one sister. All older and married. My father died last year. I've got nephews and nieces, too."

"You brung pictures with you?"

"In my wallet. I'll show you later."

"You got to see my family." Molly laid aside the little sweater and dug into her pocketbook. After proudly displaying snapshots of her three children and all the grandchildren, she picked up her knitting, saying, "My oldest daughter wants me to live with her, but I enjoy my independence. My husband died seven years ago—ah, so many widows in this world! Well, that's when I began working for the Blackburns. Scott hadn't written his first book yet."

"What did he do for a living?"

"Taught English in high school. His grandfather on his mother's side left him an inheritance, including a big house, so he could well afford a housekeeper. I was a Christmas present for his wife, bless her soul."

"Some present," said Kathy.

"Sure and that inheritance was mighty lucky for me. 'Twas my first time working in somebody else's house, but I felt at home from the first day."

"Did Scott's mother inherit, too? Or was she dead?"

"Not dead—disowned for not marrying the man her father chose for her. Being she was an only child and there were but two grandchildren—Scott and Lucy— they inherited. But Scott be more than generous to his parents."

"You've never met his sister Lucy, have you? She got me this job."

"Why sure, I met her several years ago when she came to California for a visit, and then again last year for Joan's funeral. Nice woman. Another widow. Tsk, tsk—so many widows."

"Tell me about Joan. What was she like?"

"A good woman. Home and family came first with her. And church. They'd not miss church on Sunday. But after she died, the boss stopped going." Molly shook her head sorrowfully. "They had hoped for two or three children, you know. But not till last year did she get pregnant again. And then that miserable drunk . . . oh, when I think of it!" She fell silent, and for a moment even her hands were still. Looking at Kathy, she said, "You like to go to church, Kathy?"

Kathy nodded. "And I teach Sunday school. A primary class."

"I'm not surprised. And you know something? You remind me of her. Joan. Not the face, I don't mean that. Something about you—a *niceness*."

Kathy grinned at her fondly. "You're good for my ego, Molly." She watched the rapid knitting needles with interest. "Would you teach me to knit sometime? It looks like fun. And with today's prices, I could save a lot of money knitting my own sweaters and for gifts."

"Why not. What is it you do in your spare time?"

"Write stories for children."

Molly's hands paused in their work, and she looked up. "Did you say write? You *write*?"

She looked so astonished, Kathy giggled. "That's what I said. And I just sold my second story—two hundred dollars. How about that?"

"A *writer* she!" There was a thrill in Molly's voice. " 'Tis too good to be true!" She addressed the ceiling, her eyes gleaming, "Could the man do better, now I ask you? Who could understand a writer better than another writer? A blessing right under his nose—"

"Molly, stop it!" Kathy was both touched and annoyed. "You know it takes more than that to make a marriage." She added pointedly, "Love, for instance? On the part of *both* individuals? Why do you persist—"

"And why not!" Molly interrupted her brusquely. "Don't you think I worry about him and Tony like my own? I'd like to see them be a real family again in that big house of his, and maybe another young'un or two. And to hear him laugh like he used to, from deep down in the heart. A man without mirth—like a wagon without springs, in which one is given a disagreeable jolt by every pebble over which it passes." She let out a gusty breath. "And, Kathy, I like my job, I want to keep it. Suppose he marries a bitch. Excuse the language. Or suppose there's a mother-in-law come live with them who wants to run the house? Suppose—"

"Too many supposes, Molly. You're fretting over things that might never happen."

"Well, maybe. But where else would I be finding a job like this one where I'm treated almost like family?"

"Let's pray," said Kathy gently, "that Scott will resolve his problem and find someone who'll make a good wife for him and mother for Tony, and that you keep your job."

Molly looked her in the eye. "You'll pray, too?"

Kathy nodded, feeling her face grow warm. "I want what's best for everyone. Especially Tony. I'm very fond of him, you know. Now tell me, this relative on her way here—you know her?"

"Olivia Borelli. Third cousin, I believe. Wait, I dropped a stitch." Molly unraveled a bit of the wool and got her needles going again. "Can't say I really *know* her, though I met her a few times before she married and went off to Italy to live."

"How did she meet her husband?"

"He came to the States on business mixed with pleasure, and three weeks later they were man and wife. 'Twas a quick courtship, to be sure, and I heard the Blackburns discussing it at the table. Borelli's a textile manufacturer, and I be wondering . . . would the woman have married him if he was poor? I tell you, I doubt it. With her looks, and loving expensive things . . . And now divorced. Tsk, tsk." Molly clicked her tongue disapprovingly.

"She's very beautiful?"

"With her coloring, who could deny it? Hair like fire, green eyes, milk-white skin. Makeup always perfect. And her clothes—they cost a mint." Molly pursed her lips thoughtfully. "But you know, beauty like that can be a curse. Spoils people. They get so much attention, they become self-centered. Now you, Kathy"— with a warm smile—"you're just pretty enough in a nice natural way. And I could tell when we met that you are a nice person."

"Oh, I *do* like you, Molly. Go on, tell me more about myself."

"You'll be marrying a handsome, famous author and live happily ever after," said Molly airily.

"And a one-track mind you've got for sure." Kathy stood up. "I'll see you later. Don't bother with a fancy tea. Toast with jam will be fine."

"One word more, lass. There's a funny thing about life: if you refuse to accept anything but the best, you very often get it."

Kathy kissed her on the cheek, smiling. A philosopher yet, that Molly.

*　　*　　*

When the Jeep pulled into the courtyard, Kathy was on the swing suspended from the oak; and in her shorts, with her hair flying, she easily could have passed for a teenager. She was sailing high and couldn't hop off, so she waved as the Jeep appeared and pulled into the garage side of the outbuilding.

Soon the trio came walking out and approached the swing. Scott was carrying two large suitcases and Tony a small one. Kathy's heart gave a sudden thud and began beating rapidly. So this was Olivia.

She was clad in a slim-fitting, pale yellow dress that showed off a shapely figure. Her high-heeled shoes and bag were tan. She had removed a tan silk scarf from her head, and Kathy saw that her hair was indeed like fire. Was the color real? Styled short and sleek with a side part, the hairdo hugged her head as though sculptured there. Rather than detract from her femininity, the short cut enhanced it, for it displayed a beautifully shaped head and shell-like ears. In front of the right ear was a small lock that dipped forward toward the hollow beneath a high cheekbone, just the right accent for the boyish hairdo.

Kathy slid off the swing and moved forward to meet the visitor, trying to smooth her own hair into some semblance of order. The woman was gorgeous, she had to admit, with a sleek, exclusive look that made her feel like a disheveled child in comparison.

Scott set down the luggage as he introduced them. "Olivia, this is Miss Miller, whom I've been telling you about. Miss Miller—Mrs. Borelli."

Kathy wasn't sure whether she ought to offer her hand and a second later was glad of her hesitation, for the woman's hand remained at her side.

"Oh, hello," said Olivia, her light-green eyes sweeping over her in a glance. "So you're Scott's secretary for the summer."

Kathy tried to sound relaxed. "How do you do, Mrs. Borelli. I've heard so much about you."

112

She was grateful for Tony's presence, taking the attention of the other two away from her for a moment as he lifted his left wrist for her to see. "Look what Cousin Olivia brought me, Kathy. Real silver." He was wearing an identification bracelet.

Kathy leaned over to examine the expensive present and could see it was sterling. It had "Anthony Blackburn" engraved on the nameplate. "It's lovely, dear."

"There's a little something for you in my suitcase, too, Tony," said Olivia, smiling at him. "You'll have to wait till I unpack."

"Something else? Really?"

She chucked him under the chin with a beautifully manicured hand. "I tell you what. Come to my room with me and I'll find it for you right away."

"Righto!"

"Here, let me hold your arm, Tony. This dirt yard isn't too well suited to my high heels." They walked toward the back door. Watching them together, Kathy felt a curious twinge in her heart.

"Coming, Miss Miller?" said Scott, picking up the luggage. She nodded and preceded him into the house. As the little group paused to speak to Molly, she went on up to her room. Soon she heard them go into the room across from hers.

A few minutes later, while she was trying to decide what to wear for dinner, Tony knocked on her door. "Kathy?" he called. "Look what I've got!" As she opened the door, he held up a thick paperback activity book. "It's full of word games and puzzles and mazes and stuff. Take a look."

She riffled through the pages, gratified that he wanted to share his pleasure with her. "My, what a fat book. Looks like fun. Should keep you busy for a while."

"I'm gonna do some before we eat." He scampered off, clutching the book to his chest.

Through the open door facing hers, Kathy could see Olivia talking to Scott, her lovely face upraised to his.

They were a handsome couple, the tall dark figure of a man and the exquisite titian-haired woman.

Later, when Olivia made a dramatic entrance into the living room where Scott and Kathy were having pre-dinner rum liqueurs before the fire, she was so breathtaking, Kathy felt sure a man would be able to overlook any fault she might have, seeing only the perfection of her face and figure. She had dressed for dinner in a low-cut, multi-green chiffon gown with long, flowing sleeves that were like butterfly wings when she lifted her arms. The various shades of green emphasized her white skin and deepened the color of her eyes. She wore a jade bracelet but no necklace. From her dainty ears hung teardrops in jade. Kathy was to learn she seldom wore anything about her neck, thus keeping attention focused on her face and hair. She had to be close to Scott's age, but was one of those women who came to full bloom and were most beautiful in their thirties. There were no signs of aging about her, no faint lines to mar her smooth skin, and Scott rémarked that she was lovelier than ever.

She acknowledged Kathy's presence with a nod and moved toward him gracefully, leaving a fragrant trail of expensive perfume behind her. "What's that you're drinking, Scott?" There was a husky quality to her voice that was most attractive.

"Banana-rum liqueur. We have hibiscus-rum and coffee-rum also. What's your pleasure?"

"Same as you," she said, laying a slim, white hand on his arm. Tall in her heels, she had to look up at him.

They sat on the sofa facing Kathy in her chair opposite. Scott offered Olivia a cigarette and lit one for himself, commenting that Kathy was a non-smoker. They could hear the pitter-patter of rain against the windows; and the crackling fire on the hearth was a welcome remedy for the chill in the air.

Though she could not hope to compete with Olivia's striking appearance, Kathy was glad she had worn her black ensemble, for the gold accessories dressed it up nicely and, as Pierre had said, black emphasized the honey-gold of her hair. With it again wound in a braided coronet atop her head, the princess feeling was helping to boost her self-confidence. She could see a faint surprise in the green eyes that were now surveying her as though seeing her for the first time. She pretended not to notice as the woman studied her from head to foot, but she found herself thinking the one good thing about smoking was it gave you something to do with your hands. She clasped them on her lap and lifted her chin, telling herself she shouldn't feel inferior because Olivia Borelli was more beautiful and educated and talented than she.

Olivia took a sip from her glass. "It's good. Where's Tony?"

"In his room, deep in that puzzle book you brought him," said Scott. "It was thoughtful of you, Olivia, and a fine choice. He's really enjoying it."

"I'm glad. Does he remember me, do you think? He was only—what, six?—when I last saw him."

"Your hair he definitely remembers. As who wouldn't."

Olivia crinkled her slender nose at him. "Remember how I hated the color when we were kids? Until I turned fifteen. Then my hair suddenly became an asset. I'm glad I never fooled around with dyes." Her eyes narrowed in Kathy's direction. "May I ask if you bleach your hair, Miss Miller? You have brown eyes, I see."

"It's my natural color."

"Hmm . . . very nice." Again the green eyes swept over her through a haze of cigarette smoke, taking in every detail of her appearance. It was such a thorough appraisal, Kathy felt uncomfortable, as though she were being measured as a possible rival for Scott's affection. But this woman had come here merely for a visit, a vacation—hadn't she?

As she listened to them reminisce of the past, she

gathered they had seen each other frequently while growing up.

"You've changed drastically since your teen years, Scott." Olivia's gaze slid over him like a caress. "It really struck me the last time I saw you. Isn't it amazing what time will do?"

"Thank heaven," he said with a wry smile. "I must have been the skinniest lad in town, as well as the most awkward. Tell me about yourself, Olivia. I'm sorry your marriage didn't work out."

She shrugged and blew out smoke through her nostrils. "You know those Latin temperaments. Carlo was very jealous. He hated my going anywhere without him. As though I could spend my days staring at the four walls of our house! And when we did go out together, he resented the way men looked at me. Really, he was impossible that way." She shrugged again and drew on her cigarette. "One good thing—money was never a problem. We did a lot of traveling whenever he could get away from his business, and he gave me everything. Except the freedom to come and go as I wished. You'd think he'd never even heard of Women's Lib, and, after all, I was an American wife. We quarreled about it all the time. Well, one day he struck me, knocked me clear across the room."

"He did?"

"He did, Scott, and I broke a finger as I fell. That was it, the end." She held up her left hand, from which she had removed her wedding ring. "The little finger. It healed satisfactorily—see? But I couldn't play the piano for a long time." Her expression was rueful. "It was a mistake, of course. We were wrong for each other from the start. Perhaps that's why I had no desire to have a child, though he was all for having several. A good way to tie me down, of course."

"I'd love being tied down to a darling baby," said Kathy impulsively. And could have bitten her tongue at the cold stare Olivia gave her, knowing she had said the wrong thing.

116

"Are you implying I don't like children, Miss Miller?"

"Why no, of course not." Kathy could feel hot color sweeping into her face, and wished she'd stop blushing so.

"Don't be touchy, Olivia," said Scott soothingly. "You were wise not to bring children into an unhappy marriage. Miss Miller was just expressing her fondness for them. She even writes for them—stories for the juvenile magazines."

"Children's stories?" Olivia ground out her cigarette in the ashtray. "Must be a pleasant way to earn some cash," she said lightly. "I may try it when I run out." The implication was that anybody could write for kids, and Kathy was gratified when Scott set her straight.

"I think it takes a special talent to write for children. It's not all that easy, Olivia; you don't just dash off whatever comes to mind. The young are impressionable, and what they read can affect their lives." He frowned thoughtfully. "I should think requirements for good juvenile writing would be more strict than for adults. Writing for young minds should be approached with a serious regard for the possible influence of one's words."

"Dear me, looks like I made a boo-boo," said Olivia, pouting prettily.

Kathy could have hugged Scott for his understanding. This was more like the sensitive man on his book jackets. Though he did not write for children himself, he instinctively recognized it as a specialized field and did not downgrade it as some were inclined to do, even some writers.

"What are your plans for the future?" he asked his cousin.

"Haven't thought much about it. Anyway, I've enough money to last for a while."

"And alimony?"

She shook her head, expelling her breath on a sigh.

117

"A lump sum settlement. The court case was a hassle. I'd like to forget it, if you don't mind."

"What made you come to Haiti after having returned home? Too bad you didn't stop here on your way to California. Would have saved you thousands of miles."

"I didn't learn you were here until after I got home. Scott, remember how you used to help me with my problems? You've always been a good friend and . . . well . . . I couldn't wait to see you." Sudden tears sparkled in Olivia's eyes. "Was I presumptuous? I'm at such loose ends, and I knew you were someone I could talk to, and that you wouldn't condemn me for being the fool I've been. Oh, Scott, you did try to warn me about marrying him, about the suddenness of it. But he was so charming, he swept me off my feet. I should have listened to you." A tear slid down her cheek and she hid her face against his shoulder. His arm went around her comfortingly. Watching them, Kathy felt like an outsider.

"Forget it, Olivia, it's over," he said. And giving her a little shake, "But should you meet someone else, don't rush into it next time, hear? Make sure he's right for you."

Raising her head, she gave him a tremulous smile. "Anyone in mind for me?"

His lips quirked. "Well, I know several bachelors who believe in equal rights for women."

"And do you?" she asked, arching her plucked eyebrows at him.

"To a point, Olivia. I still believe the man should be head of the home."

Molly's whistle rent the air just then, and Olivia gave a start. "Good heavens, what's that!"

"Our dinner bell," said Scott with a laugh, withdrawing his arm from her. "Mostly for Tony's benefit. You'll get used to it. Well, ladies"—he arose and waved them toward the door—"after you."

When they returned to the living room, Olivia taught

Tony a simple little ditty on the piano which he played with two fingers over and over until his father advised him enough was enough. "You can practice it tomorrow when you're alone in the room."

"Okay, Dad." Tony slid off the piano bench. "Guess I'll work on one more crossword puzzle before bed. Man, do I like that book! Thanks a lot, Cousin Olivia."

"You're welcome, dear." When he had gone, she said, "He seems to have adjusted all right to his mother's death."

"He took it well." A tiny furrow appeared between Scott's eyes. "But he never talks about her. Nor have I seen him cry. It worries me a bit." He changed the subject, and Kathy knew he didn't care to dwell on it himself. "How about playing something for us, Olivia. The 'Moonlight Sonata'?"

"That's always been one of your favorites, hasn't it." She went to the piano and seated herself gracefully. Her every movement was so feminine, so poised and perfect, Kathy suspected it was a studied grace, and that Olivia was well aware of her effect upon others, especially men.

She flexed her hands, poised them over the ivory keys, struck the first deep chord, and at once drew her listeners into the music as her slender fingers commanded the keyboard, rippling, caressing, sweeping over it with authority, producing sounds that stirred the sensibilities. Kathy felt envious as she saw how raptly Scott listened with closed eyes, as though the notes were weaving a spell around him. Olivia was extremely effective at the piano, a goddess of beauty and of lovely sounds, and Kathy wondered if she could love a man with the kind of feeling she displayed in her music.

"How beautifully you play, Mrs. Borelli," she said sincerely, as the piece ended on two quick chords. "Have you considered concert work?"

"Oh, yes." Olivia approached the table to pour herself another cup of coffee. "I majored in music, you

119

know. Thought I wanted to become a great concert artist. But it takes drive as well as talent, and many hours of daily practice. I got tired of it." She shrugged and sat on the sofa next to Scott. "I'd rather just play for enjoyment and not have to sweat over it. Frankly, I prefer a husband to a career. I need and enjoy having a man look after me, as long as he doesn't try to put me on a leash."

She looked like a fragile butterfly in her floating chiffon gown. But, somehow, Kathy couldn't help feeling there was nothing soft or helpless about Olivia Borelli deep inside. She wasn't sure why she felt this, unless it was that faculty known as woman's intuition.

As they began reminiscing of their college days, Kathy excused herself and retired to her room. She was healthily tired, but sleep did not come easily that night, and she had to admit to herself that she was jealous of the red-haired beauty.

Chapter Ten

Olivia appeared at breakfast in a glamorous lounging coat patterned with blue roses and silver leaves on a pale green background. It hugged her slim waist, falling in graceful folds about her green-slippered feet.

"Good morning, everybody." She sat down next to Tony. "This is early for me, but I thought I'd come down and join you my first morning here. What's your work schedule, Scott?"

"Nine to one. Or, rather, Miss Miller works till one. I'm usually done before that, unless I go out on research. I don't know how you're going to fill your time, Olivia. If you'd like to look around this morning, Tony can take you out on horseback."

"Good idea," she said.

"But, Dad, Marc and Louis—" Tony began.

"You can see your friends later, Tony. It's Olivia's first day here, and I'd like you to be host while I'm working. Show her the waterfall and some of the countryside."

"You don't mind, do you, Tony?" Olivia coaxed with an appealing smile.

He shook his head politely and looked down at his plate. What else could he say? thought Kathy. Olivia could have said she'd manage for herself until Scott was free to show her around. Obviously, she was the kind who expected people to cater to her and thought nothing of the boy having to postpone his plans for her benefit.

"Who are Marc and Louis?" she inquired. "Are there other white families in the area?"

Tony explained they were native children who lived in the cottage behind the house.

"And that's who you play with?" She wrinkled her delicate nose in distaste. "Really, Scott, how democratic can you get? Do you think it's wise for him to associate with the peasants? He's likely to pick up some of their ideas."

"I don't think so," he said quietly. "He realizes they're superstitious."

"I did some reading before coming here, and *really* . . ." She let her voice trail off significantly.

Scott frowned, and the gray of his eyes seemed to darken. "What would you have him do, Olivia? There's not another white youngster around here. Frankly, I'm glad he's got those boys out back to play with, or it'd be a boring summer for him." There was an edge to his voice that warned she would do better not to pursue the subject.

Molly was setting breakfast on the table, and from her sidelong glance at their guest and the slight tightening of her lips, Kathy could tell she was thinking Olivia was a snob. Scott was not, for which Kathy mentally applauded him, since she herself lived by the golden rule. Regardless of race, creed, or color, all human beings deserved to be treated with dignity and respect, and she had little patience with people who looked down their noses at others.

"Yum, French toast." Tony licked his lips. "Say, Molly, you getting that wish you mentioned two or three weeks ago?" he asked her playfully. "You do look like you dropped a couple of pounds. Right here," tapping his chest with a grin. "You really skipping breakfast every day?"

"For sure. Except for coffee."

"How can you resist French toast?"

" 'Tain't easy."

122

"It looks so *good*." He grinned at her teasingly. "Just a teeny weeny taste, Molly?"

"Taste makes waist," said Molly. Kathy laughed. The lady was not only wise but witty.

"What d'you mean—taste makes waste?"

"I said *waist,* Tony. W-a-i-s-t." Molly spelled it out for him.

"Oh. Ha, ha! Glad I don't have to worry about such things." And he lit into his food with gusto.

Olivia took only one slice of the French toast and half a sausage; and when Scott commented she ought to eat more than a bird, she remarked that the best way to ensure a good figure was to go easy with the appetite. Perhaps she gained weight readily, thought Kathy, glad she could indulge her own appetite without fear of adverse consequences. When she reached thirty, then she might have to be careful.

Breakfast over, Scott went out to saddle the horses while Olivia went upstairs to change into something suitable for riding. Tony ran to tell his friends he'd join them later, then he and Olivia rode off together.

The work session that morning went so well, Kathy dared make Scott a suggestion. He had fallen silent for a long minute, and when she asked if she could be of help, he told her he was trying to think of a way for his main character to explain the difference between the right word and almost the right word. He'd thought of one or two comparisons but had discarded them as trite.

She pondered it as he paced the floor. A bit timidly she ventured, "Excuse me, but how's this: The difference between the right word and almost the right word is the difference between lightning and the lightning bug."

A quick smile warmed his eyes. "Say, that's *good*." The keen look he gave her seemed to indicate his opinion of her literary ability had just gone up a notch, and when he said, "After this, when you get an idea, speak

123

up," she could have hugged herself for having come up with something he could use.

He dictated a whole chapter that morning, which seemed to lift his spirits to such a degree, he was unusually affable at lunch. He even discussed his work, and it was plain he loved it.

"I can't think of anything I'd rather do," he confessed. "I've always had a love for the English language and thought I'd like to teach it, which I did. Then one day I read a story in *Esquire* by a well-known author—I forget his name now. It struck me as mediocre, and I told myself I could do better. Well, it seemed a challenge and I set out to prove it. Imagine my elation when the editor of *Esquire* snapped it up and asked for more. When the second and third stories also sold, I decided full-time writing was for me. I found it exciting, satisfying, and felt I'd like to try a novel. Since money was no problem, I resigned from teaching, successfully wrote and published my first novel, and went on from there."

"A born talent!" Kathy was thrilled. "Most writers have to struggle through trial and error for years before making that first sale."

"I've been fortunate," Scott admitted. "I only wish I'd gone into it sooner. Teaching is a noble profession, of course, but everyone has his niche in life, and I've found mine."

"I guess I've yet to find mine," said Olivia ruefully. She added, her teeth glinting, "A good, comfortable marriage—that's my niche."

Comfortable? It seemed to Kathy an odd word to use in reference to marriage. She would have chosen "happy" or "loving" or "solid." One thing was certain—anyone as gorgeous as Olivia would have no trouble finding a second husband. Or a third. Kathy hoped she'd be more careful in her choice of spouse next time. A marriage, to endure, could not be based on physical attraction alone. Nor was it a game to be played over and over with different partners, although nowadays many couples seemed to go into it with that kind of attitude. The holy vow "till death do us part" was taken much too lightly. As far as Kathy was concerned, marriage was a sacred lifetime affair. If there was give and take between partners, a real attempt at cooperation, there would be no need for divorce.

"Tony showed me the waterfall," said Olivia, helping herself to the fresh fruit compote. "Pretty spot. I'm glad there's a place to swim, but I do have to be careful of the sun. I burn easily."

"I remember one time you got an overdose and were laid up for a couple of days," said Scott, his eyes flicking over her face and arms. "I've never seen skin as white and delicate as yours. Still bruise easily?"

"Afraid so." She gave him a slow smile from beneath curled, mascara-darkened lashes. "Fragile doll, you used to call me—remember? I was always getting hurt. So you see? I do need someone to take care of me."

Fragile? Somehow that wasn't Kathy's impression of Olivia Borelli, despite her slimness and milk-white skin. She sensed a core of steel within this woman. Perhaps Olivia exaggerated her fragility when men were about, but Kathy couldn't help feeling she was more than capable of taking care of herself.

"I wanted to take a path into the forest," Olivia went on. "To explore a little. But Tony said a *mambo* lives there, and that she practices black magic."

"That's what Fernand told me," Tony said quickly.

"He's not to go into the forest," said Scott. "I've heard of that voodoo priestess. She resents anyone going near her place except to buy her evil services. Decent people are afraid of her. They avoid her. I would advise you do the same."

Tony met Kathy's eyes and hastily glanced away.

"I understand it really works—the black magic," said Olivia.

Scott gave an almost imperceptible shake of his head and a half-glance toward the boy to warn her not to go on with the subject. "Many weird things are said to work in Haiti," he commented briefly. "One can't believe everything one hears and reads."

"Like pacts with the devil so black magic'll kill an enemy," put in Tony, snickering. "And zombies. Imagine anybody believing dead men walk!" He placed his napkin on the table and excused himself. "My friends want me to play a game with them."

When lunch was over, Kathy returned to the study to finish typing the completed chapter. Then she went to her room to work on her story about the American boy lost in Haiti. The house was quiet during siesta. Presumably everybody was resting. Scott had mentioned that even when he had no desire to sleep he often relaxed on his bed and let his mind wander freely as ideas sometimes came to him that way.

Kathy completed half her story and went down to the kitchen to see if Molly was up. She was, and they had another knitting session, with Kathy working on a square of blue yarn that was to be a scarf.

"Who am I knitting for?" She was thrilled to think she was working on something somebody could use.

"Finish it and it's yours," said Molly.

"Ah, thanks. It's not so hard to do, is it?"

" 'Tis a simple stitch you're doing. Oops, you dropped one. Here, let me show you how to pick it up."

They chatted and knitted for three quarters of an hour, and then Tony came in from play to ask if Kathy would read to him. He was tired and felt like just sitting and listening to a story. "I like having someone read to me once in a while. My mo—" He broke off abruptly and fiddled with his shirt, pretending to button it.

Mother, thought Kathy. His mother had read aloud to him. But he could not talk about her, not yet, any more than his father could.

They went to the study, and she pulled out a book of Haitian folk tales from one of the shelves. "Let's sit

126

on the couch," she said. "Stretch out with the pillow under your head, if you like. That's it. What was the game you played with your friends?"

"*Mayamba*. It's played with four chips of shell or baked clay. We used broken chinaware, one side of each chip white, the other blue. You can have any number of players and they all compete against the thrower. Like in dice."

"How does it work?"

"If a player throws two whites and two blues, or four whites or four blues, he wins. If he throws any odd combination, he loses. I brought peanuts for the prizes. Louis won the most. Find a Bouki story, Kathy. He's so *dumb*! Ti Malice is always putting something over on him."

"You've read from this book?"

"Yeah, three or four stories. The Bouki-Ti Malice tales are the most popular, Dad says, even though you sometimes can guess what's coming. He says they appeal to the Haitian funnybone. See, Ti Malice is sort of a con man and practical joker. Bouki has a mind that works slow and is always getting into stupid situations where Ti Malice takes advantage of him. Say Malice wants him to do something. He tells him *not* to do it, and it always works."

"Reverse psychology," murmured Kathy, smiling. "Like what, for instance?"

"Well, in one tale Ti Malice runs away from angry Bouki and gets stuck in a hole in a fence. When Bouki finds him, Malice begs him not to push him through the fence. So Bouki does, and Malice gets away, of course. Say *cric*, Kathy."

"*Cric*," she said.

"*Crac*," said he, grinning. "The storyteller starts off with *cric* and the audience replies *crac*—and that in Haiti means getting ready for a story."

"Well, live and learn." Kathy riffled through the pages. "Ah, here's one entitled *Uncle Bouki Gets Whee-Ai*. Did you read that one?"

127

He shook his head, and she began. It was about Bouki watching an old man eat his food with such enjoyment it made his mouth water. Just as he asked what the food was called, the old man bit into a hot pepper and exclaimed "Whee-Ai!" So Bouki went to market to buy five centimes worth of whee-ai. Nobody had any such thing. Then he met Ti Malice, who listened to him and told him he would get him some whee-ai. What he did was put cactus leaves in the bottom of a small sack, with a pineapple on top and then a potato. He brought the sack to Bouki. Bouki reached in and took out the potato. "That's no whee-ai," he said. He reached in and took out the pineapple. "That's no whee-ai," Bouki said. Then he reached to the bottom and grabbed the cactus leaves. The needles stuck into his hand. He jumped into the air. He shouted, *"Whee-ai!"*

"That's your whee-ai," Ti Malice said.

Tony chuckled drowsily. *"Dumb,* man! You should read the fisherman story about those two characters, Kathy. Bouki's a real fool in that one. One more story?"

She started one that was not about Bouki and before she finished, Tony had drowsed off. Finding a coverlet in the bottom drawer of the cabinet, she spread it over him. Then she sat in one of the armchairs and continued reading the folktales until time for tea. She could already smell something baking.

Molly's whistle woke Tony. He sat up and stretched. Seeing the book still on Kathy's lap he said, "Did you read the fisherman story? Yeh? Funny, huh."

"Like you said, Bouki really played the fool in that one. And he's such a *serious* fool," said Kathy, chuckling as she put the book away.

"Something smells good. Cinnamon." They went out together to the patio.

Scott and Olivia joined them a few minutes later, the constant cigarette between the latter's fingers weaving its smoky film about her head. The coordinated avocado slacks and shirt she wore fit her perfect figure revealingly, deepening the color of her eyes and accentuating the flame of her hair. She knew well the kind of clothes to wear to emphasize her exquisite femininity, thought Kathy. But, probably, she'd be enticing wearing even a burlap sack, for she had sex appeal with a capital *S*. Scott's eyes strayed to her again and again. Kathy could not help but notice, and the sunny day lost some of its brightness for her.

"An afternoon nap suits me to a T," said Olivia, after Scott had seated her at the wrought-iron table covered with a white cloth upon which Molly was laying the tea things, including fragrant cinnamon buns fresh from the oven. "In Italy I always rested after the midday meal, as do many Italians," Olivia continued. "Siesta is a good idea, really. In America we scurry about so, we hardly take time to relax, and we often gulp down our food. The Italians work hard but they know how to stop and enjoy life. And whether their meal is bread and cheese and wine, or something more sumptuous, they take the time to relish it."

"Did you like living in Milan?" Scott asked her.

"Why not? Life is pleasant there, lively and gay—cafés, cabarets, La Scala, beautiful public gardens. It's a modern city with tall buildings and vast roadways. I guess you know its economic importance to Italy, being the industrial center. Carlo's house is on the outskirts . . . Oh, well, let's not get into that."

"Have you been to Venice?" Kathy asked her, pouring the tea into their cups. "It's hard to imagine a city built on water, though I've seen pictures of it. I'd love to ride in one of those gondolas."

"Yes, Venice is beautiful, like a floating dream." Olivia put out her cigarette and helped herself to a bun. "But something is happening to that city. High tides have been causing floods. When that happens, the pedestrians crossing St. Mark's Square have to use a wooden walkway. Scientists aren't sure whether the lagoon on which Venice sits is rising up, or whether the city itself is sinking. I understand the water is advancing at the rate of about one inch every five years."

"I'd like to visit Italy one day," said Kathy. "Is it true there's an Italian style of girl-watching, especially in Rome? I read about it in a magazine article. It said that to the Roman, the way an American male watches a girl is ludicrous. The American might pretend to study his newspaper until she's almost out of sight and then glance up quickly from the corner of his eye. What's more, he may watch only one girl out of many, whereas the Roman watches *all* girls, even the older women. It's a point of honor with him—so I read." Kathy giggled. "If that's true, watching the girl-watchers must be quite a show. Have you been to Rome, Mrs. Borelli?" She could just imagine the eye-popping time the girl-watchers would have with this redhead in their sights.

"Yes, I've been there. And, yes, there is a technique to Italian girl-watching," Olivia said with an amused smile. "A woman approaches. The man stares straight into her eyes. Then he lets his glance drop to her breast, her waist, her hips, her legs—as though adding a column of figures. In fact, I believe that particular technique—and there are others—is called the bookkeeper's stare. The women don't mind. It's flattering to be reminded they are women. But they don't stare back. That's considered bold. The double standard still survives in Italy, I'm afraid."

"I suppose you speak fluent Italian," said Kathy.

"Certamente." Olivia had acquired the Italian characteristic of talking with her hands, and her gestures punctuated her speech like grace notes. Between that and the husky voice and her charm, she had a captive audience. "If you like art, Miss Miller, and do get to Italy, be sure and stop at Florence. It's such an important art center it takes several days to see all the chief sights. Italy is a beautiful country, there's no denying it. And the food! It takes will power, let me tell you, to keep your figure. All that delicious pasta of every

shape and size, stuffed and otherwise . . . Ah, well, that's over for me, and, really, it's been good to get back to the States. Another cinnamon bun, Tony? Go ahead, take it with you if you want to leave the table. See you later. Hm, I think I'll try one of those little bananas."

She fell silent, eating slowly, daintily; and Kathy saw that Scott could hardly keep his eyes off her. And who could blame him? She was so lovely, any man would be enthralled by her. Once or twice, when he met Olivia's glance, she gave him a slow, lingering look from beneath her lashes that seemed to speak volumes. Kathy began to feel like a nonentity sitting there, for they apparently had forgotten her presence. Though a quiet had fallen over them, the two were communing, and she felt excluded.

Finishing her tea, she excused herself and went to her room to finish her story. But she couldn't seem to concentrate and found herself prowling restlessly around the room. She could hear the children playing in the courtyard. She went outside and asked Tony to help her saddle the bay.

"Where you going, Kathy?"

"For a ride, nowhere special," she answered vaguely. "Don't worry, I won't get lost."

She decided to trot to Furcy and back, since it wasn't that far. But once there, she found herself going farther down toward Kenscoff. At Kenscoff she kept right on going—and when she reached Pétionville she knew she was on her way to Pierre's house.

Well, why not? Why shouldn't she visit the Frenchman if she felt like it?

Walking her bay up the driveway, she dismounted, tied him to a tree, and rang the doorbell. Pierre opened the door.

"Why, Kathy, what a pleasant surprise! You are alone?" He glanced over her shoulder as he took both her hands in his. "Ah, you came on horseback, I see.

Come in, come in, my dear." He drew her inside. "I was about to have a crème de menthe. Join me. Ah! First I must show you my rose garden. You have not seen it. You like roses, Kathy?"

"Love them. Who doesn't?"

He led her through the house and out a back door into the rear garden where he pointed out a pomegranate tree, breadfruit, papaya, and almond trees. Roses completely surrounded the lawn—red, white, yellow—and the air was fragrant with their odor. There were varieties from all parts of the world, Pierre told her proudly, including many without thorns. Kathy examined some closely, for she never had seen thornless roses before.

"Do you attend to them yourself?" she asked him.

"With the help of a yard boy."

"They're beautiful. You have a lovely place here, Pierre."

"*Merci.* Come, let us have our crème de menthe."

He stacked some record albums on the stereo and the soft music began. Then he filled two fragile long-stemmed glasses with mint liqueur, topped them with cream and handed her one. They sat down together on the sofa.

She said, "How is it you decided to live in Haiti, Pierre? Do you have family in France?"

He nodded. "My mother, a younger sister, and her two sons. In Marseilles. My sister is married to an attorney, and my mother lives with them. As for me, I managed a department store with an eye toward having a business of my own one day. Then I visited Haiti, found my opportunity here, built a nice business by specializing in Haitian handicrafts—and here I remain, perfectly content."

"Have you seen your family since you came here?"

"*Oui.* Several times. The last time I visited France was two years ago. I may go again next year. Can you dance the *méringue,* Kathy? One is playing on the

132

stereo now. It is the national dance of Haiti, you know."

"I've never danced it." She listened to the sweet melody with its light, somewhat staccato rhythm. "I like it," she said.

He stood up and held out a hand to her. "Let me show you how it is done. The music is lilting and melodic, is it not? Very distinctive. Once you have heard the rhythm of the *méringue,* you will always recognize it. It is also called the wooden leg dance. Watch me, Kathy, and you will see why," he said with a whimsical smile.

He executed the steps for her, holding one leg stiff and gyrating the pelvic joint and kneecap of the other leg. Kathy tried it, and when she'd caught on, Pierre set the needle back to repeat the melody, and they did it together, their movements synchronized.

"You learn quick, *chérie,*" he complimented. "It is rather a dignified dance, no?"

It was. There was nothing sensual about it, nor did the partners hold each other close. Kathy found herself enjoying it, once she got into its mood and rhythm. "My goodness, I never expected a dance lesson," she said, laughing. "Now I can do the *méringue*, thanks to Pierre Rollet. You're a good teacher."

"Good at teaching many things," he murmured, smiling into her eyes. He refilled the tiny glasses and sat beside her on the sofa. His housekeeper was awfully quiet, she found herself thinking. She hadn't heard a sound from the kitchen, though she could smell food cooking.

"I'm glad I came home early today or we would have missed each other," he said.

"I would have told your housekeeper I'd wait for you."

"Ah, but she would not have been here to let you in. She comes by the day. She cleans up, leaves a meal in the warming oven for me, and departs. I value my privacy."

She wouldn't have come had she known that, thought Kathy. She sipped her crème de menthe, which she had never tasted before, and tried to appear casual.

"You will stay and have dinner with me, *chérie*?"

"I really should get back before dark. But thanks for the drink and the dance lesson." She set down her glass and made a move to rise, but his hand stayed her.

"Not yet, Kathy." Putting down his glass, he brushed the back of his hand lightly across her cheek. His big brown orbs gazed into hers meltingly as his fingers traced the curve of her jaw and the smooth line of her throat, sending little shivers spiraling through her body, making her suddenly aware of herself in an almost voluptuous way. He had a tremendous faculty for making a woman feel beautiful and desirable just by the way he looked at her, his very gaze so sensual it was like a physical touch. Ah, the power of the biological urge, the attraction between male and female! She had no romantic inclinations toward this man, yet he was able to stir her senses.

She placed a hand on his chest to push him away, but his arm was around her now, slowly but forcibly drawing her close, turning her to lie across his lap with her head resting against his shoulder.

"Pretty little American," he whispered.

A pulse fluttered in Kathy's throat as he bent his head and pressed his warm lips to the hollow there, trailing kisses upward to her ear, where he murmured French endearments in a voice gone husky with desire.

She tingled beneath his caresses. He was so handsome and appealing. Had such beautiful, brown, long-lashed eyes. A pleasant languor was stealing over her, and she realized in sudden panic that if she didn't stop him now, she might not be able to later, for this was no fumbling schoolboy but an experienced lover. Never before had she encountered such a Don Juan.

"Pierre . . . please don't!" She turned her head as

his lips sought hers, and struggled to sit up. But his strong arms merely tightened their hold as with smoldering eyes he murmured, "Relax, *chérie*, do not fight me."

Chapter Eleven

The sudden chiming of the doorbell stilled the panic that had begun to beat like wings in Kathy's breast. And it served as a dash of cold water to quench the Frenchman's ardor, for his arms fell away from her, permitting her to sit up.

Thank God! she thought, smoothing her hair back and tucking her blouse more securely into her slacks. Pierre gave her a whimsical look, lifted his hands in a gesture of defeat, and went to open the door. Kathy's heart gave a leap as she heard a familiar voice, and then Scott came striding into the room.

"It'll be dark soon," he said to her brusquely. "I came down on horseback to escort you home."

He had left Olivia to come after her! He cared!

But then she remembered he felt obliged to watch over her because of her mother's request, and her momentary elation collapsed.

"I would have brought her home," said Pierre, "and the horse, too. You knew where she was—"

"I guessed," said Scott. "Evidently she rode off on the spur of the moment. Ready, Miss Miller?" He seemed impatient to be off.

Meeting her glance, Pierre shrugged. And when they bid him good night, his eyes were rueful as he bowed over her hand. *"Bonsoir,* Kathy. You will come to my shop, as you said?"

She inclined her head in the affirmative. Somehow she could not be angry with him. What had happened was partly her own fault, for she had sought him out. She shouldn't have come.

As they made their way to the main road side by side on horseback, Kathy on the smaller horse now, Scott said coldly, "There seems to be a streak of rebellion in your makeup, Miss Miller. I explained to you about that fellow. Believe me, that private domain of his is where the spider catches the fly." His glance was keen. "Perhaps I came none too soon?"

Kathy turned her eyes away from his and said nothing. She would not give him the satisfaction of "I told you so."

He went on in a stern voice, "You took a risk in being alone with a man like that. I've heard stories about Rollet, and a girl like you is hardly a match for a charming lover-boy of his type."

"What do you mean 'a girl like me'?" she said, bristling. "I'm not all that naive."

"You're obviously a nice girl. I doubt you've had occasion to tangle with someone like Pierre Rollet."

"Well, I hope you don't think he could seduce me." *Could he?* She thrust the thought away hastily.

"Stay away from his house," Scott said curtly.

"I didn't intend to go back," she snapped. And she felt impelled to add, "I wouldn't have gone in the first place had I known no housekeeper was there."

"I'm glad to hear that," he said in a gentler tone.

They were on the main road now and had to ride single file, for it was alive with two-way traffic: pedestrians on their way home from the city, tour cars on their way back from the hills. Some roadside vendors were gathering up their wares; others were eating from stews simmering tantalizingly over roadside fires. It was twilight, a time of enchantment, with purple mountains against dark-rose skies, and billowy clouds edged with pink and gold. The air was turning to velvet, and pinpoints of fire flickered like jewels on distant hillsides. The curtain of night fell quickly before they arrived home—one more reason for Kathy to be glad Scott had come after her.

That evening Olivia entertained at the piano and sang several songs, including an old Italian classic. The husky quality of her contralto voice added a sexy note to the love songs—another plus in her favor, thought Kathy, at least where the opposite sex was concerned. Truly, as Scott had said, this woman did all things well.

At least she's not a writer, Kathy told herself. That's one thing I can do that she can't. But since it was her only accomplishment, it brought her little comfort.

Though she stayed up later than usual, Scott and his guest were still chatting when Kathy retired. They never seemed to lack subjects for discussion—their privileged childhood, their college experiences, the foreign countries they had visited—topics in which Kathy could not participate other than to ask an occasional question or make some brief comment. She had listened with interest, but it was so beyond her limited small-town experiences, she could not help but be aware of her naiveté, which in sophisticated company seemed to her a failing.

In the days that followed, Olivia slept late mornings and had her breakfast served in bed, which did not endear her to Molly. And though she was friendly to everyone when Scott was about, she paid them little mind during his absence unless she was bored and in need of company or a favor.

To Scott she was always sweet and charming, always very feminine, even a little helpless in his presence. She had a way of treating a man, of magnifying his masculinity, that was gratifying to the male ego. Perhaps more women should adopt her techniques, Kathy found herself thinking. Most American women were inclined to be self-sufficient, proud that they could equal the opposite sex in so many areas of life—which, of course, was a thorn in the side of the male chauvinist. But Olivia—had she learned the technique in

Italy?—flaunted only her feminine virtues of beauty, charm, and sex-appeal, leaving the man to shine when it came to matters involving cleverness and intellect—thus proving herself the clever one.

It didn't take long for Kathy, or Molly either, to perceive that Scott had been caught in the soft net of the woman's spell, and that she was weaving it about him subtly yet determinedly, with the intention of winning his love. And Kathy could not blame her, for they were well matched both in background and cultural level. Perhaps this was the woman to help him start a new and happy life, she thought wistfully. Olivia was doing exactly what Molly had said a woman must do in Scott's case, and who was Kathy to object when she herself had refused to set her cap for him.

There was something itching at the back of her mind, however. And it must have been nagging at Molly too, for it cropped up in discussion one afternoon during a knitting session.

"You be noticing she's after him, Kathy?"

"Yes, I've noticed."

"To tell you the truth, I don't like that woman."

"What do you mean, Molly?"

"I got a feeling she's not what she appears on the surface. Like an actress she is—every gesture is planned."

"Calculated, you mean? I've had that same feeling."

"A woman can tell. But not him. He'll not be seeing past that pretty face of hers. She's out to get him, Kathy, and she's all wrong for him."

"You don't know that, Molly. They grew up together, have the same background. She might be very good for him." Kathy was trying to be fair, though it wasn't easy.

Molly's hands grew still. "I've a notion . . ." Her voice trailed off. She chewed on her bottom lip. "Seems strange . . ." Again she left the sentence dangling.

"What seems strange?" Kathy prompted.

139

"That she should come all the way here to be with him. After just returning to California from Europe." Molly spoke slowly, as though weighing her words. " 'Tis a long journey from California to Haiti. After six years, she couldn't wait till September to see him?"

Kathy's hands ceased knitting also, and she waited expectantly. Somehow she knew Molly was going to voice the very thing that had been bothering *her*.

"I don't care, I'm saying it! I think she decided to go after him before she even arrived here!" The words came out in a rush, and a weighty pause followed, during which the two women stared at each other.

"And that means . . ." Molly began.

"That it's calculated and without love," Kathy concluded.

Molly nodded, her face grim. "He's handsome, rich, famous—a wonderful catch for any woman. And she must figure, like you said, that they have a lot in common. But without love? No! Not for Scott. Not for Tony. Oh, I wish I knew why she and Borelli divorced!"

"He was jealous, she said."

"Aha! Could be he had good reason."

"Now you're guessing, Molly. We're judging her on guesses, and it really isn't fair."

Kathy laid a hand on Molly's arm and said gently, "Do you suppose having to keep her breakfast warm and serve her in bed has made you biased?"

"Well . . . maybe," Molly admitted. " 'Tis a queen she thinks she is. And haughty-taughty when he's not around to see." She compressed her lips and resumed knitting at a furious pace.

"You know, it's possible she's falling in love with him." Kathy spoke up with reluctance. Why was she defending a rival? In trying to be fair, one could carry it too far.

"That type of woman loves me, myself, and I." Molly narrowed her eyes and laid aside her knitting the better to concentrate on the subject. "I was wondering—Italians don't divorce easy, you know. Could it be Borelli was the one who wanted the divorce? She'd not admit it, of course, even if it be the truth."

"Are you suggesting she's an adulteress, Molly? Isn't that the grounds for divorce over there?"

Molly just looked at her with a shrug. Then she said, "She been pumping me about you, Kathy."

"Me? Whatever for?"

"Wanted to know how long you have been here, how you like the boss, whether he takes you out—that kind of thing."

"And what did you tell her?"

"That you came here to do a job and you're doing it. Listen, Kathy, you're rivals, you two, and she knows it. To a woman like that, every other woman is an opponent. I'll lay wager she's got few women friends, that one. I get bad vibrations from her."

Molly clapped her hands together in an attitude of prayer and rolled her eyes heavenward. "Please God, she's not the one for him. You and I know it. Make him know it, too."

"How can you be so certain?" Kathy chided her. "I still think we're judging her prematurely."

Molly's lips tightened stubbornly. "I size up people pretty good. Wait. You'll see."

One thing Kathy did see a short while later. Heading for the study to look up something, she pulled back quickly from the doorway, for inside was a couple locked in a tight embrace. Head lowered, her heart tripping, she tiptoed away to the patio and sank onto the chaise longue, closing her eyes against a rush of tears. Probably Scott had tried to suppress his male instincts, as with Kathy previously, but this time the woman was actively pursuing him, and if she persisted . . .

Oh, God, don't let him give his heart to her! I love him.

It was true. She did love him. Why else this inner ache at seeing another woman in his arms. Why else

141

the lift in her heart when he called her by her given name or smiled at her. And that wistful feeling whenever she thought of him as lover and husband. And that dream of being his bride that had filled her with such joy.

What she felt for Scott Blackburn was not purely physical, was not simply an infatuation. She loved him dearly in every way. She wanted to help and comfort him, make him happy, work with him, spend the rest of her life with him—and it mattered not whether he was rich or poor.

And now what? She was no match for Olivia.

When they joined Kathy on the patio for tea, she found herself searching their countenances. Scott appeared bemused, and Olivia seemed to glow. Kathy's heart sank. He had not rejected her. Olivia would not let herself be defeated. Did he find her so irresistible he was drifting with the tide, come what may?

Scott, I'm here, too, and I love you!

Olivia was murmuring into his ear, claiming all his attention, her titian head like a brilliant flower upon the graceful stalk of her neck. It seemed to Kathy her manner had undergone an almost imperceptible change. There was a tinge of possessiveness in how she looked at him, a lingering intimacy in the hands that touched him.

And he? Totally engrossed in her. Dazzled. Kathy felt despair as her eyes swept over the clinging yellow shell and shorts that revealed delectable curves from shoulders to ankles. Olivia had *everything*. Who could compete with such a woman?

The food stuck in Kathy's throat. She forced down some tea, so as not to draw attention to herself, then murmured an excuse and left the table. In her room she lay staring up at the ceiling with dry burning eyes, trying not to think. After a while she dozed off.

She awoke to a persistent tapping on her door. Blinking the sleep out of her eyes, she was surprised to find it was Olivia.

142

"I'd like to talk to you." Olivia brushed past her before she could open her mouth, and turned to face her. Kathy closed the door and waited uneasily.

"So you saw him kissing me." Olivia came straight to the point. "I caught a glimpse of you in the doorway." And as Kathy stared at her, she went on coolly, "You're infatuated with him, aren't you. I could see it in your eyes during tea whenever you looked at him. Too bad, Miss Miller; it must be painful to feel for someone who doesn't reciprocate." There was no sympathy in her voice but rather a touch of mockery.

Kathy felt waves of heat surging through her body. Was she really so transparent? It was too embarrassing. And the way Olivia used the term "infatuated"—as if to make light of her love for Scott.

"You're from New York, Miss Miller?"

She inclined her head, reluctant to trust her voice.

"May I ask what your father does for a living?"

Kathy cleared her throat. She did not feel like talking to this woman, but she couldn't be rude. "He was a bookkeeper for a furniture store. He died last December."

"I see. And you're not long out of college?"

"I never went to college." Kathy had a feeling she already knew that.

"You've traveled?"

Unable to be anything but honest, she admitted Haiti was her first trip. And wondered where the questions were leading.

Olivia regarded her silently for a moment, an enigmatic smile on her lips. Then she said, "Were you aware Scott's father is a titled Englishman? *Sir* Laurence Blackburn. And his maternal grandfather was a United States senator, you know. As for myself, my father is a scientist; my mother, a language professor." Her smile was frankly disdainful now. "Do I make myself clear, Miss Miller?"

Kathy seethed within and dared not speak for fear her anger might cause her to sputter.

"If I were you, Miss Miller, I'd go home before I started dreaming impossible dreams."

"I have a job to do." Kathy choked out the words. The audacity of the woman!

"I'm sure I could take your place without too much trouble," purred Olivia. "I don't intend leaving here until Scott does. Nor do I think he'll want me to," she added confidently.

"I was hired for the summer and I intend to stay and finish my work," Kathy managed to say evenly.

"Stay then." A low laugh mocked her. "A lot of good it will do you."

For a moment their eyes locked, green eyes cruel with amusement, brown eyes full of resentment. Then, with a contemptuous swing of her body, Olivia sauntered out of the room.

Kathy flung herself on the bed and punched her clenched fists into her pillow.

Later she caught sight of Olivia and Scott from her balcony. They had been strolling and were approaching the courtyard. Olivia had changed into a flowered pantsuit with a matching stole and her hand was tucked into the crook of Scott's arm. The sun was low on the horizon, and already the brief twilight was fading into night.

They paused in the yard beneath the oak. Kathy could hear the murmur of Scott's voice and the woman's soft, throaty laughter. From beneath the branches she could see them standing close together, Olivia's face a white moonflower upturned to his. Their voices drifted into silence, and even as she watched, Olivia's arms circled Scott's neck and drew his head down to hers. Their figures merged, and Kathy knew she shouldn't be watching, yet she remained motionless in the hope of seeing him push the clinging form away. He did not. When their lips parted, Olivia murmured an endearment in French and nestled her head on his shoulder. At that Kathy crept numbly into her room and quietly closed the French doors.

"What's the matter, Kathy?" It was Tony, meeting her at the top of the stairs on their way to dinner.

"Matter? What could be the matter?"

He peered at her quizzically. "You were looking ever so miserable."

"Was I?" She made herself smile, and reached for his hand. "I was thinking thoughts, that was all."

"What sort of thoughts?"

"Silly thoughts, Tony. Not worth talking about."

"You're not getting tired of being here?"

"No, dear. I like my job."

"I'm glad of that." He gave her hand a quick squeeze. They were at the bottom of the stairs now and could hear voices from the dining room. "Come into the study a minute, Kathy," he whispered. Wondering what it was about, she followed him in. He turned to face her and said, "I didn't want *her* to hear. Kathy, I wish she'd go home."

"Mrs. Borelli?" It surprised her. "I thought you liked her."

"I did. Thought I did. But things have been different since she came," he said glumly. "Dad's got no time for me, she's always with him. And I don't think she wants me around when they're together."

"Why do you say that, hon?"

"Aw, she sends me on errands. Or tells me to go work on my puzzle book. Once she told me my friends were looking for me, and they weren't. Another time when she and Dad started off in the Jeep, I ran after them wanting to go too. He didn't hear me calling, but I'm almost sure she did. And she didn't tell him to stop and wait for me."

"Could be she didn't hear you," Kathy suggested, wanting to ease his anxiety.

He frowned. "She half-turned. I think she heard me, all right. But she likes being alone with him, doesn't she?"

Since it was obvious even to him, Kathy could not deny it.

He looked perplexed. "She likes him much more than a cousin should."

"She's only a distant cousin, Tony. That makes it okay."

"Oh. Well, I wish she'd quit hogging his time," he muttered. Then his face brightened. "Say! She's been here about two weeks. That's right, she'll be going home soon."

"Uh, they're waiting for us," Kathy reminded. She hadn't the heart to tell him that Olivia intended staying the summer.

As they went into the dining room, she saw that Olivia had usurped her place at the table next to Scott. Tony spoke up at once. "That's Kathy's seat," he pointed out, as if she didn't know.

"It doesn't matter, Tony, I'll sit next to you," said Kathy. Since the two were involved in a romance, they might as well sit together at table.

Molly noticed the change in seating immediately, and she transferred the meal from the cart to the table with tight lips and undue clatter and stamped out of the room muttering darkly to herself.

Olivia stared after her with her eyebrows almost touching her hairline. "What's the matter with her?"

Though Scott looked surprised himself, he made an attempt to defend Molly. "We all have our moods, Olivia. You'll have to excuse her."

"Moods? From the hired help? Really now!" She sniffed and tossed her head.

The meal was an ordeal for Kathy. Though her intellect acknowledged that Scott and Olivia were now a twosome, her heart could not accept it as final. Did Olivia love him, or was he merely a wonderful catch, as Molly had suggested? Did he love Olivia, or was he so vulnerable she could twist him about her finger?

Whatever, there was an aura of intimacy about them that made Kathy's heart ache. Even her head was throbbing. Scott noticed, for he said, "You're looking pale tonight, Kathy. Don't you feel well?"

Kathy. Again. She thrilled to the sound of her name on his lips, and his concern was like wine warming her insides. "I've a bit of a headache," she admitted, giving him a wan smile. "I'll take something for it after dinner."

"You look as though you need a good night's rest." Olivia's voice expressed sympathy, but it belied the quick flash of triumph Kathy saw in her eyes. The woman was well aware of her inner turmoil. She was crowing over it.

Perceptive Molly. She had sized her up correctly thus far. Perhaps her other assumptions about Olivia were also correct.

"You going home next week, Cousin Olivia?" Tony asked her. He made it sound like a casual question, but Kathy knew what he hoped to hear.

"Home, Tony?" Olivia's white teeth caught at her full lower lip, and she frowned pensively. "Well, I'm staying with my parents for now, but I don't consider it home. And, actually, my mother and I never did get along. But until I decide what I'm going to do . . ." A helpless little gesture of her hands. Clever woman, thought Kathy. She already had decided.

"To tell the truth, Tony dear, I hate leaving here," she continued wistfully. "It's been wonderful being with you and Scott, and it's done me a world of good already. I've been able to relax and almost forget . . ." Her voice trailed off pathetically, and a tear glistened in her eye. She looked so wistful, Scott rose to the bait at once.

"You're welcome to stay as long as you like, Olivia. We're here till September."

"I was hoping you'd say that. Thank you, my dear." She lay a hand over his, with a quick glance at Kathy as if to say, What did I tell you?

Kathy made a pretense at concentrating on her food. Olivia knew how to get her own way, that was for sure. On top of everything else, she was a good actress. There was no end to this woman's talents.

147

Noting that Tony looked none too happy, Olivia remarked shrewdly, "Perhaps you feel I've been monopolizing your dad's time, darling? But, remember, I've been away so long and we've had so much catching up to do. I tell you what—let's spend a whole day together soon, the three of us. Maybe go out of town, someplace where we can just relax and enjoy ourselves for a whole day."

The three of us. That, of course, excluded Kathy. Just as well. Watching Olivia and Scott together for a whole day wasn't exactly her idea of a fun time. But again her champion went to bat for her.

"Kathy makes four," he pointed out.

"Don't count on me, Tony," she said hastily. "I really don't know what I'll be doing at the time. I've things to catch up on, letters to write, a story to finish." She pushed back her chair and stood up. "I'll go take that aspirin now and get to bed early. Good night, everybody."

And that took care of that. She wouldn't have wanted to go with them had Scott himself invited her, and she wiped at the foolish tears that blurred her vision as she mounted the stairs.

That night she concluded her prayers with: "Lord, take care of Scott and Tony. I want them to be happy . . . so please see that things work out for their good. And for my good, too, whatever that might be. Amen."

It gave her a measure of comfort and she was able to fall asleep.

Chapter Twelve

As the days erased each other one by one, and Scott's temperamental bouts decreased in number, Kathy began losing hope that he one day might look at her with eyes of love. It appeared he was falling in love with Olivia, for they were constantly together. She had woven her net of enchantment securely about him, and gave the impression she loved him too. By now she was calling him darling.

Molly was not convinced it was love on *either* side. "With the boss 'tis infat—what be that word, Kathy?" It was siesta, the house was still, and they were having coffee together in the kitchen.

"Infatuation."

"That's what it is, I'll wager. She could charm any man, to be sure, but that don't mean it's love."

"You have to admit he isn't as quick to lose his temper. He seems happier." Tears gathered unexpectedly in Kathy's eyes, and she lowered her head.

"Oh, Kathy, child, you *do* love him. Why don't you fight for him?"

Kathy sniffed and brushed at her tears with her hand. "What good would it do? I can't compete against Olivia. Besides, she's more his kind than I am. At first I suspected everything she said and did was an act— but, Molly, she does seem to care for him. And they're very compatible. He seems more relaxed, doesn't he? And she's planning an all-day outing for Tony's sake, and things just seem to be going so well," she concluded, her voice choking a little.

"Humph! I'm not convinced she's sincere, that one. Olivia Borelli is and always will be number one, I'll wager. And all that sweetness when he's around? Hah! He doesn't know how haughty-taughty she can be, especially to the 'hired help.' And maybe yesterday while you and the boss were working you heard her play the piano?" Kathy nodded and Molly continued, "Tony went in and asked her to teach him a little ditty. She wasn't in the mood. My door was open and I listened. Sure and I'm nosy, but only because this family means something to me. He kept after her—you know how kids are. She told him to quit pestering her, and she called him a brat. A *brat*—a nice lad like him!" defended Molly indignantly.

"It must have been one of her bad days," said Kathy, giving her the benefit of the doubt. "We all say things we don't mean, you know that. She probably apologized later."

Molly shrugged and changed the subject. "There be company for dinner tonight. Mr. Rollet. You had dinner at his house, so now it's our turn. Would you like corn muffins for tea, Kathy?"

"That would be fine, Molly." So Pierre was coming. Between his charm and Olivia's, it should be an interesting evening.

He arrived in a yellow station wagon a little after six. From the living room Kathy could see the car through the front window as it pulled into the driveway. Scott and Tony were on the porch. A minute or two later, Scott ushered his guest into the living room.

Kathy had on a long-sleeved, flower-print dress, and her hair was parted on the side and plaited into a single thick braid that lay forward across her right shoulder. Over her left ear she had pinned a scarlet hibiscus. Pierre's eyes expressed admiration as he bowed over the hand she extended from her chair.

"*Bonsoir,* Kathy, my dear," he said, and seated himself in the other armchair. Freshly shaven and cologned, he had on a charcoal leisure suit with a rose-colored shirt open at the throat. Again she had the impression he had just stepped out of a bandbox, and the perfect fit of his clothes suggested they were custom-made.

Scott wore his gray suit with a white sport shirt. Comparing the two men, Kathy thought how attractive they were, each in a different way. Scott was the taller and had the kind of quiet good looks that grew on one (although they had affected *her* from the start), whereas Pierre's romantic handsomeness hit you all at once, with instant emotional appeal.

They heard the tap-tap of heels across the mahogany floor of the hall, and Olivia appeared, pausing in the doorway so that it framed her like a picture. All eyes swung in her direction. The men rose.

"Hello, everybody," she greeted in that appealing voice of hers. She was wearing her multi-green chiffon gown. Poised there, with her hands on her hips so that the long full sleeves resembled wings, she made a lovely ethereal impression. And undoubtedly was aware of it, thought Kathy.

Something flickered in Olivia's eyes for just an instant as they lighted on Pierre's handsome face. Then she was coming forward into the room, bringing with her the fragrance of Chanel No. Five.

"Olivia, this is Pierre Rollet," Scott introduced them. "He runs a gift shop in the capital and lives in Pétionville. Mrs. Borelli is from my home town in California, Pierre. She's vacationing with us."

"*Bonsoir,* monsieur," Olivia murmured, giving him her hand.

He raised it to his lips. "*Enchanté,* madame."

Seeing him eye the ringless fourth finger of her left hand, she held it up, saying, "I'm no longer married. So what's the point in wearing a wedding ring."

"No point." He flashed his white teeth at her.

"Do call me Olivia. Let's not be formal." She helped herself from the cigarette box on the coffee table. "Are you married, Pierre?"

151

"I prefer to remain free as a bird," he informed her candidly, with a disarming smile. Reaching for the lighter, he held it to her cigarette, his eyes intent upon her face.

Observing them together, Kathy saw them as two of a kind. Both sensual. Both beautiful, graceful, elegant. As a couple they were a knockout. But that was wishful thinking. Olivia and Scott were the couple.

The Frenchman's gaze was still on Olivia's face as she sat down next to Scott on the sofa. He blinked, as though coming to himself, and sat down. "Forgive me for staring, but, truly, you are most beautiful." There was a tinge of awe in his voice.

Olivia laughed softly, exhaling a cloud of smoke. "*Merci*, Pierre, that's always nice to hear. And I'm used to being stared at. Ask my cousin here."

Scott shrugged, his lips quirking at the corners. "It's always been that way. Women, too, stare at her. One does get used to it. We grew up together, you know, and she was always an eyeful." He arched a quizzical eyebrow at her. "I'm not sure yet whether it's gone to her head."

Kathy couldn't help envying Olivia's poise. Had a man stared at *her* with such intensity, she would have blushed to the roots of her hair. But Olivia took admiration for granted. No stupid blushes. No getting flustered. Kathy couldn't imagine her stammering with embarrassment under any circumstance. That air of elegance and sophistication—*I'll never have it.* How could one appear sophisticated with a face that turned all shades of red at the slightest provocation.

They had pre-dinner sherry, and when the conversation turned to Pierre's shop, he said to her, "If you are interested in Haitian paintings, Kathy, I recently acquired some very fine ones. I carry only quality merchandise, no tourist junk. Truly creative work, skillfully designed, for forty percent to sixty percent below what you would pay in the United States—free port prices."

"Sounds good. And I'd love to have at least one native painting depicting Haitian life." She turned to Scott eagerly. "Could I borrow the Jeep after work tomorrow, do you suppose? I'd fill it with gas. I do want to send some gifts home, and here it is mid-July already." Surely he couldn't object. The shop was a public place—not like going alone to Pierre's private domain.

He nodded. "I've made no plans for the Jeep tomorrow. But try to be back by dark."

"If I may have a sheet of paper, I will sketch a street map showing the easiest way to get to my shop," said Pierre.

Kathy went to get a sheet from the study and watched over his shoulder as he drew a few simple lines leading to the store, which he marked with an *X*. "It is on Grand Rue. Take a left on the Pétionville road to Avenue Panamericaine, also known as Avenue John Brown. See here? It will take you to Grand Rue. Then turn left and you cannot miss my shop. There is a large sign outside: ROLLET'S HAITIAN GIFTS.

"Thanks, Pierre. The map will come in handy. There's Molly's whistle."

The American steak dinner was followed by a variety of fruits and nuts and then coffee in the living room. During dinner, while Scott was busy conferring with Molly about something, Kathy had thought she caught a flirtatious glance passing between Olivia and Pierre. When she witnessed the same thing in the living room, it was with a sense of shock. The first time she might have imagined it, but now she realized Olivia was sending out signals to let Pierre know she found him attractive.

She kept discreet watch after that from beneath her lashes and could not help but notice the subtle body language: pregnant glances, arched eyebrows, intimate smiles. Shocked, she could not comprehend how a woman serious about one man could at the same time flirt with another.

153

The signals were discreet, hardly noticeable unless you were looking for them—which she was, and Scott was not. Besides, Tony kept drawing his father's attention to himself throughout the evening, and Olivia took advantage of this to communicate silently with Pierre. Kathy pretended not to notice, but very little escaped her.

Olivia played several classical pieces on the piano, and Pierre's enthusiastic applause expressed sincere admiration for her talent. Then she sang *Je Vous Aime*, and Kathy felt sure she was singing as much to the Frenchman as to Scott, and that Pierre was aware of it. Because Scott enjoyed listening to music with his eyes closed, he missed seeing the intense and searching quality in the Frenchman's eyes whenever his gaze and Olivia's met during the love song, which she half-crooned, half-spoke, in the sexy manner of a French *chanteuse*.

Growing more and more indignant, Kathy pretended to listen with *her* eyes closed, but, unlike Scott, she was watching the couple from beneath her lashes, and the more she observed, the angrier she became. Not so much at Pierre as at Olivia, for he had no idea this woman and Scott were a twosome.

Tony ambled about the room during the song, looking at the pictures on the walls, touching this figurine and that, obviously bored but reluctant to go to bed.

At the conclusion of Olivia's song, Pierre breathed, "*Bravo!* I did not expect to be entertained as well as wined and dined." And to Scott, "A delightful evening, I must say."

"My dad can play the piano," Tony spoke up in an effort to get his father to share the limelight. "Play something, Dad."

"I'd hate to follow Olivia's expert performance," Scott demurred.

"Why don't we play a duet," Olivia suggested, making room for him on the piano bench. "Remember that oldie, 'Barcarolle'?"

He joined her and played bass to her melody, and this time Tony sat down and listened. It was plain he was proud of his father. When the piece ended, he approached the piano with, "Now my turn. Play 'Chopsticks' with me, Dad."

Olivia gave him her seat. "I'd like to stretch my legs. You don't mind, do you, Scott? I'll show Mr. Rollet the grounds while you and Tony have fun with the piano."

Pierre followed her to the door. He hesitated. "Would you care to join us, Kathy?" he invited politely. She shook her head, knowing full well Olivia desired to be alone with him, and vice versa. Besides, an idea had swooshed into her mind; there was something she had to do.

Since she had heard Tony play "Chopsticks" before, she knew he wouldn't take offense if she did not remain to listen. As soon as she heard the front door open and close, she excused herself and hurried up to her room. Slipping out onto the balcony, she moved the little bench she used when drying her hair in the sun and placed it where a branch of the oak tree provided concealment. Then she sat down and waited, her heart tripping. It was a lovely night of full moon, and she could see between the leaves into the courtyard below.

It pained her to resort to spying, but she couldn't let that woman pull the wool over Scott's eyes. And so she waited until the strollers rounded the wall and came into the yard, where they paused beneath the shadows of the oak. The trunk shielded them from Kathy's gaze, but she could hear the murmur of their voices, though she could not distinguish all the words.

Then she heard Pierre's breath catch in his throat. Followed by a thick silence. She did not have to see with her eyes to know they were in each other's arms; she could almost *feel* it. How *could* she! After having kissed Scott beneath this very tree!

She gritted her teeth, hardly daring to breathe. After

a while, she heard Pierre say hoarsely, *"Mon Dieu!* You are too much, *chérie."*

Another pause.

With her heart pounding, Kathy crept into her room and took a moment to compose herself. No time now to think; she had to get downstairs before those two returned.

Scott and Tony were still fooling around at the piano. Kathy went over and leaned against it, and Tony announced happily, "Dad's been teaching me a duet I can play with one hand, while he plays with two hands. Let's start over from the beginning, Dad." They ran through it for her, and the youngster beamed when she applauded.

"He's a quick study." Scott ruffled the boy's hair affectionately. "Remind me to teach you the bass part, Tony. Ah, the others are back. And you, my boy, had better get to bed now."

"Thanks for letting me stay up, Dad. Good night, everybody."

Scott passed cigarettes around and lit one for himself. "He seemed to feel a need to be with me tonight. I hope no one minded."

"Not at all," said Olivia with a smile. Tony had unwittingly done her a favor, provided camouflage for her little game with Rollet. Kathy longed to shout out the truth about this woman, open Scott's eyes to what she really was. But, of course, she couldn't do that. It was something he had to find out for himself. *Please, God!*

He poured rum drinks. Kathy declined and stood up. "If you'll excuse me, I think I'll get on to bed. And I'll see you at the store tomorrow, Pierre."

She couldn't wait to get to her room and undress and relax. It had been a tense evening for her. Olivia and Pierre—two of a kind, indeed. First he had given Kathy the eye—and now the redhead. And was he still seeing that Chinese-Haitian? No doubt he could handle several women at one time, had he a mind to. She'd hate to fall for a man like that, and yet she couldn't help liking him. Not only for his charm but for his honesty. When Olivia asked if he were married, he had told her he preferred *to remain* free as a bird. Two very honest words right there that he could have omitted. And at the dinner at his house that night, in front of his girl friend, he had made it clear he enjoyed his bachelor status and intended keeping it that way.

No, Pierre did not resort to subterfuge, and you had to give him credit for that. God only knew how many hearts were broken and lives wrecked because of empty promises of love and marriage by philanderers such as he. But that was not his style, and Kathy could not help but like him for it, though his mode of life might be contrary to her own high moral standards.

As she washed her face and got into her pajamas, she found herself forming romantic conjectures as to why he was still single at his age. Did he shun marriage simply because he enjoyed variety in women? Or perhaps something in his past had soured him against matrimony. Had someone he loved broken his heart, run away with another man? Or it could be he had suffered the painful lingering death of a beloved young wife and vowed never to risk going through such heartache again?

She sighed and got into bed. There could be any number of reasons why he avoided giving his heart exclusively to one woman. That last conjecture—too sad. She hoped that wasn't it. But any one of those guesses—except the first—put him in a more pleasant light, added some depth to his character and provided reason, if not excuse, for his philandering.

As for Olivia, she had brought something into this house that was not here before. A touch of evil.

Evil? Perhaps that was too strong a word. Deceit, then. Molly had sensed the insincerity almost from the start. An extremely perceptive woman, Molly. Those vibrations she talked about . . . Kathy had to smile. But vibrations or no vibrations, she definitely possessed the faculty for sizing up people correctly. Olivia was not for Scott, despite all they had in common. Marriage to her could only end in heartache. This was a *femme fatale* who enjoyed her power over men, and she played at love as though it were a game. No wonder her husband had been jealous. And no wonder he had tried to curb her freedom and keep her at home.

Yes, it *could* be that Borelli had caught her in the middle of a love affair and had been the one to file for, or request, the divorce. That might explain the lump sum settlement rather than the usual alimony. As for Italians not being prone to divorce—well, adultery was grounds anywhere, wasn't it?

Oh, Scott, you don't know what you're getting yourself into! Please don't let her fool you.

Dazzled by her beauty and charm, he was blind to everything else about her. Olivia was extremely clever. And a capable actress, among other things. Damn her many talents! She would make certain he'd not see her flaws and weaknesses until after they were married— and marry him she would, for this was a siren who knew how to get what she wanted. And even then she would keep her flaws hidden as long as possible, Kathy felt sure. She had had a good thing going in Italy, married to a wealthy industrialist who gave her everything money could buy. She had been able to pull the wool over his eyes for years, but perhaps had cuckolded him once too often.

Kathy realized she was conjecturing, for she had no proof Olivia was an adulteress. Yet all her instincts warned her it was true, especially after tonight. But even if this flirtation with Pierre went no further, she was bound to hurt Scott in the end.

He mustn't marry that woman.

What can I do to save him from her? she thought despairingly. What can I *do!*

Chapter Thirteen

The question must have resolved itself in Kathy's sub-conscious during the night, for she awoke with a definite solution in mind: fight for him. Molly had recommended that even before Olivia arrived. At that time the idea of chasing after a man repulsed her.

Now it was different. She *loved* him, was sure of it, no more doubts. And he was in danger of having his heart broken. Two excellent reasons for putting her pride aside and doing what she could do to save him from an unscrupulous woman.

Molly believed Kathy was the right woman for Scott—and Molly was usually right. Dare Kathy believe it also? His happiness meant more to her than her own; she wanted to give rather than take from him. Surely a love that put him first could never bring him harm.

As for their backgrounds, she might not come from elite society or have a college education, but she was no dummy—and they did have their work in common. Another thing, she loved Tony. And he was fond of her. Surely they could be happy together, the three of them.

She lay meditating on it, and the more she thought about it, the more excited she became. Until the realization hit her that she'd have to compete against Olivia in several areas, not just one—beauty, charm, and seductiveness—which put a damper on her enthusiasm. Could she possibly hope to succeed? With her lack of sophistication and her tendency to blush at the slightest provocation—what if she made a jackass of herself?

No, she mustn't think that way! Be positive—or forget the whole deal.

In the matter of sophistication and charm, she'd had enough time to observe Olivia's style. Perhaps she could emulate it. Come to think of it, she hadn't done too badly in high-school plays. Put that slight ability to good use now.

Beauty? Makeup undoubtedly could do wonders for her.

Seductiveness? Ah, that was the hard part that went against the grain—to be deliberately provocative, coquettish. She hated the very thought of being so calculating. But it was for Scott, and that strengthened her resolve. Again she could use Olivia as her model. Those sidelong glances, intimate smiles, brushing of hands.

Sighing, she sat up in bed. She had to try. She had to draw Scott's attention to herself as a desirable woman, jolt him from Olivia's spell. He had noticed her before, and she would make him notice her again. If only she had taken Molly's advice sooner. It was going to be more difficult now that Olivia had a head start. She could only hope it wasn't too late, that what he felt for Olivia was of the flesh and not of the heart, as Molly believed.

Going to her wardrobe, she selected the outfit she had worn the first day she arrived in Haiti. The white dress brought out her tan and deepened the velvety brown of her eyes, and the red beads and earrings gave a nice touch of color. As she arranged her hair in a single thick braid down her back, she planned her itinerary for the day.

First, her work. Then off to Pierre's. After that, a boutique for a glamorous outfit or two. And makeup. She needed mascara, eyeshadow, eyeliner—things she never had used before. In a way, transforming herself was going to be fun. And perhaps a revelation. After all, even Olivia's startling beauty wasn't all natural.

At breakfast she reminded Scott about using the Jeep; and when Tony asked to go along for the ride, she told him he was welcome.

Scott gave her a searching glance. "I hope you don't feel you have to take him because he's the boss's son."

"Of course not. I'd love having him for company." There was no mistaking her sincerity. "We get along fine—right, Tony?"

"Righto. I'll bring some change and buy you a treat, Kathy."

"Thanks, dear. And I'd like to leave as soon as possible, so let's not dawdle at lunch."

They passed several boutiques she decided to try on the way back. She found ROLLET'S HAITIAN GIFTS without any trouble. The map had been a good idea.

Several customers were in the store, and both Pierre and a mulatto assistant were busy. He greeted her and Tony warmly and suggested she look around until he was free to help her.

It was not a large store and did not stock in quantity. Many of the items were one of a kind, such as sculptures in mahogany two and three feet in height. Everything was obviously quality merchandise and had a price tag on it; no bargaining here. Glancing through a stack of oil paintings, Kathy drew out one depicting natives walking barefoot to market with baskets of fruits, vegetables, and chickens on their heads; and there were also children, several animals, and a roadside stand in the scene. Some fourteen by seventeen inches, the painting was entitled *Pétionville Road* and was so familiar to Kathy and so typically Haitian, she could not resist it. At eighteen dollars it seemed a steal. Although you could get cheaper paintings at the street markets, this one was exceptionally well done and a bargain at the price

Tony lounged outside the store part of the time

while she selected gifts for her family: fine sisal handbags for the women, handpainted ties for the men, and straw sandals and gayly decorated maracas for her nieces and nephews. And a sisal luncheon set for Mrs. Clark.

When she had paid the bill and advised Pierre where to send the gifts, they spent a few minutes chatting between customers. "I'm glad I came," she told him. "From the looks of your merchandise, you handpick much of it, don't you."

"All of it, my dear. Craftsmen who live in Port-au-Prince bring their wares to the shop so I can make my selections here. But I also scour the hills to see what I can find. Tourists shopping in my store save time and their nerves because they do not have to sift through a lot of junk to find quality goods. It is worth paying a little more, *oui*?"

"*Oui*." Remembering how it was at the roadside markets, with merchants calling to her, pulling her this way and that in competition with one another, Kathy realized she had thoroughly enjoyed shopping in the peace and quiet of Pierre's store. The open-air markets were picturesque, to be sure, and one should not miss them, but they were noisy and tiring.

"Another thing, Kathy," he said, "mine is one of the few shops dealing only in Haitian handicrafts. It seems to me that a tourist giving a gift from Haiti wants it to be something Haitian, no? The foreign imports they buy are mostly for themselves. I do not import, but I have an export outlet in Miami, as I told you."

A group of people entered the store, and she did not detain him. They said their good-byes, with Pierre thanking her for her patronage and assuring her her purchases would be shipped to the States without delay. It was all so casual and friendly, you'd never dream he had tried to make love to her, thought Kathy humorously.

Outside, Tony treated her to a bottle of soda from a nearby mobile vendor. She drank it eagerly, for it was

162

hot on the city streets. "Thanks, dear, that hit the spot. You know, I can't wait to get back to the blessed coolness of the hills."

"You done shopping?"

"Not quite. I want to stop at the stores on Avenue Panamericaine. Patience, Tony, I know this isn't very exciting for you."

"I don't mind. I don't get down here all that often."

In one of the boutiques she found a stunning caftan; in another, a black stretch-nylon jumpsuit that fit her like a second skin. Sexy. She purchased it, though reluctantly, for it seemed ideal for what she had in mind.

Next, cosmetics, an exotic French perfume, and home.

Kathy found her hand shaking as she tried to apply her makeup, uncertain as to whether she could pull off her little game. But if she thought failure, she would surely fail, and so she gave herself a pep talk and began again.

It was a good thing she had started early, for it took a long time for her to apply the new glamorous façade. The end result amazed her. She hardly recognized the woman in the mirror as the Kathy Miller whose wholesome good looks could pass for those of a school-girl. This creature in the silky multi-colored caftan with her shadowed lids and mascara-darkened lashes—they looked longer now!—*could* compete with the beauteous Mrs. Borelli.

She leaned toward her reflection, fascinated by the eyes. With the brows and lashes darkened and the lids faintly green, they appeared deep and mysterious; and the brown liner drawn across and beyond the edges of the upper lids gave her eyes a slightly oriental cast she found rather intriguing.

Really, this change in her appearance was more, much more, than she had anticipated. She hadn't dreamed cosmetics could make such a difference. A dusting of powder and a light lipstick were all she'd ever used. Now even her mouth looked different, like a crimson flower in full bloom.

She brushed her hair smooth and shiny and caught it to the side with a gold clip so that it flowed forward over one shoulder. Gold pendant earrings, a gold chain necklace and bracelet, and she was ready.

When the dinner whistle sounded, Kathy waited until she heard Olivia leave her room across the hall, and then waited a few minutes more. This time *she* would make the late entrance.

Nerves set in on her way down the staircase, and she felt her insides go weak. She paused, gripping the banister like a lifeline, and reminded herself of the splendid image in her mirror. It bolstered her ego enough to give a lift to her chin and to her backbone. She looked stunning tonight. She couldn't fail, she mustn't.

They were all at table when she made her entrance, and four pairs of eyes, including Molly's, stretched wide at the sight of her. Something else besides amazement flared in Olivia's green orbs for just an instant—a touch of panic? Well, like it or not, the redhaired beauty was going to have competition.

"Woweee!" Tony made no attempt to conceal his admiration. "You look like a movie star, Kathy."

"Why, thank you, Tony."

Scott seated her without a word, but there was a look of wonder in his eyes he couldn't quite conceal.

"My heavens, what a transformation!" There was a quick dagger thrust in Olivia's stare, though she was careful to keep her voice pleasant. "It's like Cinderella at the ball."

Kathy decided to treat it as a compliment, though she knew the remark was meant to be demeaning. She could not let Olivia get under her skin and still retain her poise. So she said sweetly, "Thank you, Mrs. Borelli. Coming from one so beautiful, I consider that a great compliment." To so gracious a reply, she

164

thought triumphantly, Olivia couldn't possibly make a barbed comeback without sounding catty.

Unable to contain her delight, Molly burst out with, "You look like what Tony said—a movie star. You agree, Mr. Blackburn?" she added slyly.

Scott cleared his throat and said gallantly to include Olivia, "With two such lovely ladies at my table, I'm quite overwhelmed."

Molly winked at Kathy on her way out, as if to say, "Carry on," and Kathy could feel her self-confidence mounting. So far, so good.

In the other room, she took her favorite seat near the fire and concentrated on sitting and moving gracefully at all times. She found it helped to think of the glamorous reflection in her mirror as that of an actress playing a part. Tonight, in place of conventional little Kathy Miller, she was a beautiful, graceful, lovely lady who looked like a movie star. *Hang on to that, Kathy, girl.*

As usual, she listened much and spoke little, for only by sounding off did one reveal one's ignorance. Every now and then Scott gave her a look that seemed to say he found it difficult to believe this was his secretary sitting across from him. Once or twice she dared give him a slow lingering smile. But the moment his lips curved to respond, Olivia diverted his attention to herself. Still, Kathy felt her campaign had got a good start, and by evening's end she congratulated herself on giving a better performance than she had thought possible.

In the morning she darkened her brows and lashes but omitted the eyeshadow and liner, which she felt were more appropriate for evening wear. She donned her snuggest slacks and a scoopnecked blouse of pink crochet that clung to her breasts, exposing the cleavage just a bit.

In the middle of dictation Scott's voice suddenly faltered. Looking up, Kathy saw him eying her décolleté neckline, which was what she'd had in mind when she selected this particular blouse. Their glances met. He turned away. She waited for him to collect his thoughts, feeling a wee bit embarrassed, yet smiling on the inside. He was aware of her, all right.

Later on in the day, she went to the kitchen carrying a pair of pointed barber scissors for Molly to use on her hair. The ends were beginning to look ragged, and she asked her to trim it for her.

Tony was having a drink of water and remarked, "Now Louis can have that piece of hair he wanted. And I got a tiny box to put it in." He went to get it.

Kathy sat a bit away from the table, and Molly draped a cloth about her shoulders. Withdrawing a nailclipper from her pocket, Kathy began cutting her fingernails, complaining, "They grow like crazy, my hair and nails both."

"You want me to cut straight across?"

"Yes. And no more than two inches, please."

"Oh, there you are, Miss Miller. I'd like to talk to you." Olivia had entered the room. "A haircut? I'll wait."

Drat the woman! She was the last person Kathy wanted to talk to, and she could guess what it would be about. Keep your cool, she reminded herself.

Olivia lounged against the wall, the smoke from her cigarette spiraling about her eyes, giving them a veiled look. Having her watch made Kathy uncomfortable and she tried to ignore her as she clipped her nails.

Molly trimmed her hair slowly and carefully and stepped back to view her handiwork. "Ah, nice and straight. Good sharp scissors. The ends they look thicker now." And as Tony reappeared, "Take what you want, Tony, before I sweep. But why should you give Louis some of Kathy's hair?"

"Because he asked for it. He likes the way it shines in the sun." Tony gathered some from the floor, tucked it into a small cardboard box and took off again.

Molly proceeded to sweep up the scraps of hair with

dustpan and brush. "I have things to do in here now. Everybody shoo, please."

Olivia glanced at her disdainfully and snubbed out her cigarette in the sink. "I'll 'shoo' because I wish to speak to Miss Miller in private and *not* because you order it."

Molly's back stiffened. "A request it was."

"You're in no position to order, request, or anything else," snapped Olivia. "And you've never learned your place, obviously."

Molly turned away with her lips clamped into a thin line, and Kathy knew it was to keep herself from snapping back at the "haughty-taughty" woman. Poor Molly. She'd be out of a job for sure if Olivia became Mrs. Blackburn. It was plain the two women disliked each other, and Olivia would manage somehow to get the housekeeper fired—even if it took subterfuge. *All the more reason for my campaign,* thought Kathy.

Olivia followed her upstairs to her room and closed the door behind them. She came to the point at once as they faced each other. "Just what do you think you were up to last night? Frankly, you amaze me. I never would have guessed you'd have the nerve to attempt to steal my fiancé from under my nose."

"Fiancé? I wasn't aware you were engaged."

"It won't be long, I assure you. We've already discussed marriage."

Kathy's heart skipped a beat. Had it gone that far already? Or was this woman lying. She wouldn't put it past her. "Look, Mrs. Borelli, since you already know I care for him—"

"And *you* know he cares for *me,*" Olivia cut in, her eyes flashing.

"I've tried to believe you love him, Mrs. Borelli, and that you'd make him a good wife because of your similar backgrounds. But after seeing . . ." Kathy hesitated.

"Seeing what?" Olivia demanded.

"Seeing you flirt with Rollet the night he came to

167

dinner, that's what!" The words tumbled out resentfully.

"So you were watching me, were you?" Olivia could not deny it, so she made light of it. "So I flirted with him. So what? It meant nothing." She stared at Kathy, her face catlike, as though she were assessing the degree of danger in this adversary. There was a brief silence in which Kathy could hear the piping of a bird outside. Then Olivia's lovely mask fell back into place as she regained her composure. She said coolly, "Keep your nose out of my business, Miss Miller. I'm going to marry Scott Blackburn. Is that clear?"

Unable to contain her defiance, Kathy retorted, "Good luck. May the best woman win."

Olivia, turning toward the door, seemed to freeze. Her expression was hidden from Kathy, but the air suddenly seemed charged. Kathy found herself holding her breath in the few interminable seconds before Olivia opened the door and walked out of the room.

Kathy shut the door behind her and leaned her back against it, her hands clenched at her sides. The more she saw of the woman, the more she was convinced she would bring only unhappiness to Scott and Tony. So what if she flirted with Pierre? How *could* she make light of such a thing—to consider herself practically engaged to Scott, yet feel free to carry on with another man! It made Kathy's blood boil.

Tony's voice penetrated her thoughts from out in the hall. "But when *are* we going on the outing, Cousin Olivia?"

"Don't bother me now."

"But I've been waiting *days*—"

"So wait more days. I've got more important things on my mind than a damn outing with you!"

Kathy heard a door slam shut. Then came Tony's knock. She let him in, and it was obvious he was upset, though he tried to conceal it.

"Louis thanks you for the hair, Kathy. He sent you something to wear around your neck." He withdrew a

168

small wooden cross from his pocket and handed it to her. It was crudely carved and varnished, suspended from multicolored braided yarn. "He made it himself—to sell, I guess—but he wants you to have it."

"How nice of him—for a measly scrap of hair. Thank him for me." She placed it on the dresser. "Sit down, why don't you?"

He slumped into the rocker, and she sat on the bed facing him. "You're feeling pretty low, aren't you?" she said gently. "I heard what Olivia said to you in the hall."

"Looks like there won't be any outing. Aw, shoot! I was counting on it, a whole day with Dad."

"You might still go."

He shook his head gloomily. "She doesn't really want to spend a whole day with me. Heck, she doesn't even *like* kids."

"How do you know?"

"She's only nice to me when my father's around— that's how I know. I think she wants to marry him. She better not," he added darkly, and stood up. "Think I'll go for a walk."

There was a forlorn look about him that wrung Kathy's heart. "Want company?" she suggested softly.

His smile was tremulous. "Sure . . . if it's you," he said.

For her campaign that evening, Kathy squeezed into the black stretch-nylon jumpsuit. Zippered down the front, it had a mandarin collar, long full transparent sleeves, and bell trousers that hugged her thighs and flared out below the knees. Observing herself in the mirror, she couldn't help but flinch a little, for it fit like a glove, revealing every line and curve of her body. But she did look chic; and black was stunning on a blonde. Anyway, she wasn't Kathy Miller tonight. She was that glamorous movie star.

She brushed her hair into a high ponytail held by an elastic band, and covered the elastic by winding a lock of hair around it. Next, her pendant gold earrings and bracelet, and a gold brooch pinned to one shoulder. Low jeweled sandals. Several dabs of the new French perfume.

Feeling a bit too self-conscious to make a grand entrance, she went down to have a pre-dinner sherry with Scott. His eyes flickered when he saw her, and one eyebrow arched quizzically. Did he think her snug outfit daring? At least he was noticing her, and that was the purpose of it.

Olivia was late for dinner, and Tony didn't appear at all. Molly informed them he'd taken a tray upstairs. And the way Molly eyed Kathy's jumpsuit, she had a feeling the housekeeper didn't approve of it.

Olivia swept in as they started the first course, looking like a dream in a creamy low-cut nylon gown, her titian hair gleaming from a recent shampoo. Her glance raked over Kathy quickly, but she didn't look too perturbed at what she saw; in fact, there was a cat-that-swallowed-the-canary look about her that made Kathy uneasy.

As Scott seated her, Olivia caught hold of his hand and said teasingly, "Since I missed my drink, darling, I'd be glad to settle for a pre-dinner kiss." She tilted her face upward, and he bent over and touched his lips lightly to hers, and she murmured with a little laugh, "I guess that'll have to do for now." And she gave Kathy an amused glance as if to say she really wasn't worried about the competition because she had the game in the bag.

But Kathy was determined to follow through. As it turned out, it was an evening she would never forget.

She used every trick of Olivia's she could think of—sidelong glances at Scott, warm intimate smiles, graceful poses—meanwhile marveling at this new boldness in her. But of course this wasn't Kathy—it was that glamor gal in the mirror. *She* could get away with it.

By now Scott had to realize she and Olivia were in

serious competition with each other over him, and he appeared a bit bewildered by it all. But Kathy was satisfied with the way things were progressing, for he seemed every bit as intrigued by her as by Olivia. In fact, he couldn't keep his eyes off her, as though fascinated by her metamorphosis.

But then she made her big mistake. Scott had lit a cigarette for Olivia, and as she watched how gracefully the woman held it between her fingers and how it added to her sophisticated air, she thought: Anyone dressed as I'm dressed and playing the part I'm playing would surely smoke. It looks so elegant.

And she said to Scott, "I think I'd like a cigarette, please." There was nothing to it, surely. You simply drew in the smoke and exhaled it. Just the sophisticated touch she needed. Besides, it would give her something to do with her hands.

He frowned a little as he leaned over her chair to light it for her. She took a puff, trying to be nonchalant about it. To her consternation, the acrid smoke made her choke, and threw her into a paroxysm of coughing that shook her slim form from head to foot, and she could feel her face turn tomato-red.

Scott thrust his handkerchief into her hand, and she clapped it to her mouth. Over her hacking she heard Olivia say, "Poor dear, she's been trying so hard to imitate me and now she's gone and spoiled it. All for your benefit, you know, Scott darling. I do believe the girl has a thing about you."

"Hush, Olivia! I'll get some water."

But Kathy was running out of the room, thoroughly crushed and humiliated. She'd done it, made a fool of herself! Because of a miserable cigarette.

She flung herself across her bed and let the tears flow. What an idiot she must have seemed, and Olivia had compounded it. But she had only herself to blame for undertaking something so foreign to her nature. It was all very well to pretend she was someone else, a glamorous movie star, but it was Kathy Miller who was undergoing the humiliation.

Molly had advised—no, don't blame Molly. She had suggested only that she keep Scott aware of her as a woman, as Kathy Miller—not as a carbon copy of Olivia Borelli. Ah, that was her mistake. Doomed to failure, even without the cigarette. From the beginning it must have been obvious she was emulating Olivia, and although her striking appearance *had* attracted Scott's eye, deep down he must have thought her a little fool. That quizzical look, the arched eyebrow, the frown as he lit the cigarette for her . . . She couldn't bear to think of it! It all seemed so cheap and shoddy now. Even childish.

Oh, if only her assignment were over so she could go home and try to forget him!

Chapter Fourteen

Tony and Kathy were the only ones to show up at the breakfast table. Olivia was sleeping late, as usual.

"Dad has a headache. I like you better this way, Kathy," Tony told her. "You looked great the other night, but it didn't seem like you."

"I know. I like me better this way, too." She was glad he hadn't been around to witness her humiliation last night.

Molly referred to the jumpsuit as soon as he left the table. "You went overboard," she commented, sitting down with her.

"I'm a fool." Kathy admitted it meekly. "I even tried smoking a cigarette and almost choked to death."

"I saw you run upstairs crying."

"You must have X-ray vision. You don't miss a thing, do you?"

"Not much." Molly was frank about it. "I figured she was the one to upset you, so I went out to the hall and listened. Sure and on purpose. And you know what she was saying to him? That he should send you home and let her take over your job!" Molly's voice quivered with indignation. "He refused, of course. Told her your work was excellent and he had no reason to fire you. He scolded her for suggesting it. So she apologized—and made love to him to soften him up. I could hear them. She's not all that sure of him, Kathy, or she'd not be trying to get rid of you. Hang in there, lass. There's still a chance, and I'm still praying."

A chance? Kathy sighed. It seemed unlikely.

"He stayed up last night drinking by himself," Molly continued. "Don't you see what that means, lass? That he's still troubled in his soul . . . and *that* could mean he hasn't opened up to her about that problem of his. When one loves, one shares—true? Once he gets things off his chest, he'll feel better and things will change for him. Sure and I think so. Oh, but not with that one, please God!" Molly crossed herself fervently.

"She told me they've discussed marriage already," said Kathy glumly.

"Maybe so. Maybe not." Molly gave her an encouraging pat on the shoulder. "Look, you have to remain here till September. Stay sweet, lass, and I'll lay wager the blinders will be falling off the boss's eyes by then. Tony's getting wise to Olivia already. His papa will be next, you wait and see."

Kathy gave her a wan smile and went back to her room to answer the latest correspondence from her mother. It seemed she had joined a senior citizens' group and was keeping active with volunteer work and short trips with her new friends. At least things at home appeared to be going well.

On her way out at nine o'clock, she heard Tony's voice coming from Olivia's room. The door had been left ajar and he was speaking in a loud, agitated voice. She found herself pausing to listen, thinking she was getting as bad as Molly where eavesdropping was concerned.

" . . . and you better not 'cause I don't want you for my mother! Bet you'd try and have me sent away to boarding school if you could!"

"And what's wrong with boarding school?"

"I want to be with my father!"

"You're the one who mentioned boarding school, not I. And you've got a nerve sounding off to me like this, you little brat! Who do you think you are, ordering me not to marry your father. Who needs your permission?"

Kathy felt rooted to the spot and wished Scott could

hear for himself this woman's callous attitude toward his son.

"I'll tell him not to marry you. I-I'll tell him you hate kids." Tony was beginning to sound desperate.

"You will, will you? Of course he'll know you're jealous—I'll see to it. Now get out, I haven't finished with my hair. No! Wait a minute, Tony." There was a brief pause. "Hey, look, I'm sorry." Olivia's voice had changed; there was honey in it now. "Let's be friends, Tony, huh? After all, if we're going to be living to- gether—"

"No, we're not!"

Kathy backed into her room and left the door open a crack.

"And you're *not* gonna marry my dad!" she heard Tony's parting shot, and then his feet running down the hall. A door slammed on the other side of the house. He had retreated to his room.

Kathy unclenched her hands. She glanced at her wristwatch. A few minutes late for work. Reluctantly, she went down, praying no comment would be made about last night's fiasco.

Dictation had no sooner got underway, than there came a tap on the door and Olivia walked in looking on the verge of tears. "Forgive me for interrupting . . ." Her lips quivered and her voice broke. "I-I've been talking to Tony . . ." Tears filled her eyes. She could not go on.

Her act—and surely it was an act—took Kathy's breath away. And suddenly she understood. Expecting Tony to make accusations against her to his father, Olivia had beat him to it and was going to twist the matter so as to make the boy appear in the wrong. How diabolically clever she was!

Scott took both her hands in his, his face creased with concern. "My dear, what's wrong?"

"Your son . . . he doesn't seem to like me anymore. He practically told me so." There was heartbreak in her voice and an expression of sad bewilderment on her face that Kathy yearned to wipe off with a swift right to the jaw. "Darling, he hates that you and I . . . H-He's upset about our going together." Olivia's voice caught on a little sob. Scott's arms went around her comfortingly. She burrowed her head into his shoulder, saying huskily, "Oh, Scott, I'm afraid he's picked up some queer ideas about me. You don't suppose someone has turned him against me?"

Lifting her face, she flicked a glance toward Kathy, then turned her head the other way with another pathetic little sob.

Her histrionics astounded Kathy. She was superb, a natural born actress. No wonder she had Scott fooled. He was patting her on the back like a father trying to comfort a hurt child, murmuring, "Hush, Olivia, don't cry. There's been some misunderstanding. I'll have a talk with him."

"I wish you wouldn't, darling. He'll know I came to you, and you know what kids think of squealers. It'll only make things worse between us." She paused thoughtfully, her pearly teeth worrying her lower lip. "Scott . . . do you suppose he's jealous of me?" She planted the seed with a catch in her voice. "Poor kid. He must think I'm taking you away from him. That must be it. After all, he had you to himself before I came." She brushed a tear from her eye. "Promise you'll be understanding if he comes to you about me? Don't scold the poor dear." She drew in a deep breath and pressed her cheek to his. "I do feel better for having talked to you about it. See you later, huh?" And with a rueful glance toward Kathy, "Don't mind my bringing it up in front of Miss Miller. I'm sure she knows how Tony feels about me." Kathy caught the barb in her words, but saw that it went over Scott's head.

He's bewitched, she thought dully, tears aching in her throat as the door closed behind Olivia. Utterly bewitched and completely oblivious to the fact that she was manipulating him and his household to her own advantage. What would it take for him to see the light?

She was tempted to tell him the truth about Olivia, but an inner voice bade her be cautious. If Olivia could plant a seed of jealousy about his son, think how much more easily she could do so when it came to a secretary who already had made a fool of herself over him.

Ten minutes later, glancing toward the windows, she saw Fernand leading the bay horse out of the stable. Following the direction of her gaze, Scott stepped to a window and watched Olivia mount and ride off.

As soon as she had transcribed her shorthand notes, Kathy went looking for Tony. She found him lying down listlessly in his room. "You been here all morning?" She sat on the bed with him. "Care to talk? Might make you feel better."

"Nothing'll make me feel better—till *she* goes," he muttered. "Kathy"—he sat up, and she saw how unhappy he looked—"if Dad marries her . . . I-I'll run away!"

"Oh, no, Tony. Don't talk like that."

"I mean it! Could I, could I come live with you?" He gripped her hand as though it were a lifeline.

"I'd love having you with me, Tony, but not as a runaway. You can't do that to your father. You're all he's got."

"He's got *her*."

"But you're his flesh and blood, darling. It would break his heart. Listen"—she put an arm around his shoulders—"they're not married yet, right? And you believe in prayer? Your mother was one to bring her problems to the Lord, I'm sure. You do the same, darling."

"My . . . m-mother?" He stared at her, his face working, his eyes filling with tears. And then he was in her arms, clinging to her, sobbing his heart out.

Kathy held him close, feeling her own eyes become wet. Were these the first tears he had shed since Joan's death? If so, she was glad he could cry. At last he was able to release the painful emotions he had kept bottled up inside him for so long.

When finally he dried his eyes, he gave her an unsteady smile and confessed, "I've been pretending she was still alive . . . that she'd gone on a long vacation and would be back." He made a helpless gesture and his eyes filled again. "She loved the Lord and read her Bible every day, and I know she's with Him. I guess that's better than being on vacation, isn't it? But I miss her, Kathy."

"I know, dear," she said softly, her arm going around him again. He sat quietly against her, and she felt his body relax.

Lifting his head, he looked into her face and said, "Kathy? You love my father?"

It was so straightforward a question, she could only reply in like manner. "Yes, I love him," she said simply. "And I love you, Tony."

"Me, too," he admitted shyly. "Did you tell him, Kathy?"

"No, dear, it's up to the man to speak up first."

"Well, I'll tell him I'd like for him to marry you," he recommended ingenuously, eagerly. "Then we can all go home together when we leave here."

It was such a naive and hopeful suggestion, Kathy found herself laughing with tears in her eyes. "Oh, Tony," she said, her voice slightly choked up, "if only it were that simple. But you can't, you mustn't say anything. I'd be embarrassed to death. Besides, it takes love on both sides to make a marriage. Your father loves—thinks he loves—Olivia."

"I'll tell him what she's really like," threatened Tony.

"I doubt that would help. He doesn't see her the way we see her, and it would be your word against hers. She can make him believe anything."

"So what do I do? Just pray?"

"That's what Molly and I are doing. But we've got to have faith." She sighed. "That's what I need, more faith. Molly believes it's all going to work out. And you know something? She's very often right."

It was hotter than usual. Kathy slipped into a thin nightgown and lay down for siesta.

When she awoke, she went to the wardrobe for something light to wear. She pulled out a pair of white shorts and looked for her lavender polyester blouse. She couldn't find it. Again she searched. It wasn't there. Funny. She seemed to recall packing it, but perhaps she was mistaken. She chose a white blouse, and then sat at the writing table to work on a new story until tea time.

At tea Tony mentioned he was going to ride to Furcy and back before it got dark. He enjoyed being on horseback, and it would give him something to do.

"May I go with you?" Olivia asked, her quick glance at his father suggesting she was trying to make up with the boy. Scott nodded his approval, and Tony shrugged without replying, obviously reluctant to take her along but there wasn't much he could do about it.

When they returned from Furcy, he joined Kathy in her room where she was working at the table. "I've got something to tell you," he began, a note of excitement in his voice. "Mr. Rollet was at Furcy buying somebody's carvings, and Cousin Olivia made a date with him. For day after tomorrow, Sunday, in the afternoon—just the two of them together at his house. Shoot, if she loves my father, she shouldn't be visiting another man, right? Dad should know about it. He won't like it, I bet. Maybe he'll get good and mad and send her home," he concluded hopefully, heading for the door.

"Tony, wait! Could you have misunderstood?"

"No way." He faced her with a devilish glint in his eyes. "We tied our horses outside the store, and when she spotted Mr. Rollet she told me to get lost for a little while. So I walked away, sneaked back and listened from behind some bushes. No mistake, man!"

"Tony, you didn't!" Had they all become spies because of Olivia? Oh, if only she'd change her mind about Scott and go home voluntarily!

"I've got to tell Dad, Kathy. This may be our chance to get rid of her."

"Wait a minute. Listen. I'm with you, you know that, and I'd be more than glad to see her go. But do you know what will happen if you tell your father about this and he confronts her with it? She'll simply deny making a date with Rollet. She'll say you made it up because you don't like her and don't want her here. She'll know how to handle it, believe me, and will make you look bad."

"So we should let her get away with meeting another guy?" Tony protested. "Mr. Rollet offered to come to the house and pick her up in his car, but she said she'd rather ride down on horseback. I don't think he knows about her and Dad. Does he, Kathy? You think he knows?"

"I doubt it. Tony, what if your father just happened to drop in on Pierre while she's there?"

"Huh? Oh!" A gleam lit his eyes. "Yeah, I see what you mean. Show, don't tell." He lapsed into silence, and Kathy could almost see the thoughts whizzing around one after the other inside his head.

He snapped his fingers. "How's this! I'll ask Dad to take us for a ride in the Jeep and before he can say no, you second the motion. You could say you'd like to see some of the mansions in Pétionville. We'll steer him past Mr. Rollet's house—and he'll see our horse parked outside!" he concluded triumphantly.

"We'll try it," Kathy said breathlessly.

Though she was in no mood to go out that Sunday afternoon because of a headache, she joined Tony in persuading Scott to take them sightseeing in Pétionville. Olivia had disappeared on horseback, and Tony casually remarked they might bump into her on the way.

They took Kathy to see the Cabane Choucoune, a nightclub with a huge, conical thatched roof, and some of the luxury hotels and fine homes. And then Tony slyly suggested a route he knew would lead them past the Rollet residence, and, sure enough, tied out front was their black-maned bay, telltale evidence of Olivia's whereabouts.

Scott's foot hit the brake and released it, and his arm went out to keep Kathy from striking the windshield. "Sorry," he muttered. The sight of the horse had momentarily flustered him.

He stepped on the accelerator and turned homeward, his jaw set like granite. Kathy glanced over her shoulder at Tony, who made a victory *O* with thumb and forefinger.

Home again, Scott shut himself into the study to await Olivia's return. She sauntered in near six o'clock, and he called for her to join him. Kathy and Tony hovered in the hall hoping for a showdown.

They could hear his voice raised in anger, though the only sentence they caught was the first explosive one, "What the hell were you doing at Rollet's place!" It was sharp enough to penetrate the closed door. After that his voice came through like the rumble of distant thunder, interspersed by Olivia's soothing tones, undoubtedly giving him some sort of plausible explanation.

The eavesdroppers returned to the living room, lest they be caught at it, and sat down to await the outcome. Kathy's hopes began fading as the minutes crawled by. The pain in her head became a pounding.

"She could charm a tiger, if she put her mind to it," Kathy worried aloud. "Probably told him she was riding by and noticed Pierre's nameplate on his lawn and dropped in to see his house. No doubt she was there all afternoon, but she'll say she was out riding most of that time." She emitted a soft sigh. "You'd better not count on her leaving here, Tony."

She was right. Olivia confirmed it by confronting

them. Her eyes blazed, though she managed to keep her voice under control so Scott wouldn't hear.

"So you two suggested a ride through Pétionville, eh? Some coincidence!" She stabbed a look at Tony that revealed she was aware he had listened in on her conversation with Pierre in Furcy. "You think I don't know what you have in mind, Tony boy? And you too, Miss Miller. Well, forget it, I'm not going anywhere! And Scott's simmering down already, I'll have you know. You want him for yourself, Miss Miller, but he's mine—get that through your head once and for all!" And with that, she turned on her heel and marched out of the room.

Kathy and Tony exchanged subdued glances.

"So what did we accomplish, Tony? More trouble, perhaps." She sighed and rubbed her forehead wearily. "This headache . . . I think I'll take a couple of aspirins and get to bed early. Tell Molly I'm not hungry, will you, and not to bother about dinner for me."

"Kathy, we're not quitting, are we? We can't let her marry Dad."

"I . . . let's sleep on it, shall we? Maybe tomorrow we'll think of something."

Like what, she mused gloomily as she climbed the stairs. Olivia had them beat no matter which way they turned.

Tony fidgeted throughout lunch the next day and spilled his milk on the tablecloth. "Sorry," he mumbled, mopping at it with his napkin.

"One would think you had ants in your pants," reproved Olivia. "What's the matter with you?"

"Sit still!" his father ordered as he knocked over his glass again, this time empty.

Kathy sensed the boy was bursting with suppressed excitement; and when he threw her an appealing glance, motioning with his head toward the door, she understood he had something important to say to her.

182

He had arrived late for lunch, and there had been no chance for them to talk.

She finished her juice and excused herself from the table. He joined her in the hall shortly. "Let's go to your room," he said in a conspiratorial whisper. "I got news for you."

She paused in the bathroom to take an aspirin. "The headache's back," she told him. "It's tension, I guess."

Behind the closed door of her room, he faced her eagerly. "You told me to pray, remember? Well, last night I prayed extra hard—and, Kathy, I got an idea. To tell Fernand about Olivia. I talked to him this morning."

"Tony, you didn't! Our private business? Oh, dear." She sank into the rocker, her eyes reproachful. "What did you tell him?"

"That she wants to marry my dad, that I don't like her and she doesn't like me or you either, that she's not a nice lady and I don't want my father to marry her, I want him to marry *you*. I told him everything."

Kathy groaned. "Tony, *why* did you tell Fernand all that? It's so personal. And what did you expect him to do?"

"I thought he could give me some advice or something. He's my friend, Kathy. And am I ever glad I talked to him!" He squatted at her feet and lowered his voice, his eyes gleaming. "You know what he told me? He saw Olivia go into the forest a couple days ago. That path that leads to the *mambo*!"

"Oh?" Kathy sat up straighter in the rocker.

"He followed her, wondering if she knew who lived there. She knew all right, 'cause I told her. And that voodoo lady understands English, Kathy. Fernand couldn't hear what they were saying, but he saw Olivia give her a little package, and it was his guess she was buying a spell to be put on somebody. Why else would she be there? Of course, if he'd thought it was for one of us, he would have warned us."

"Tony! Surely Olivia doesn't believe in witchcraft any more than you do?"

"Maybe. Maybe not." Tony narrowed his eyes, looking suddenly older and wiser than his years. "You remember what she said at lunch one day? That she'd heard black magic really works? Could be she's willing to give it a try."

Kathy gnawed her lip. "I find it hard to believe."

"We gotta search your room, Kathy. For a death *ouanga,* just in case. Fernand says so. He knows she's your enemy, just from what I told him."

Kathy stared at him for a long tense moment. Black magic was a lot of bunk, he'd said. Yet anxiety for her was written all over his face. And though she herself wasn't all that sure she believed in black magic . . . hadn't she witnessed unexplainable things at that *canzo* ceremony?

She nodded. "It won't hurt to look, I guess. But what do we look for?"

Tony shrugged. "Whatever we find that doesn't belong here. Some charms are like little stuffed pouches, Fernand says. But we're to be careful if we do find one. It's better you don't touch it. Why don't we let Fernand search? He'll know what to do." He added, making his tone casual, "Might as well be on the safe side—righto?"

After he'd gone, she rose from her seat and paced the floor. Was it possible? That Olivia would stoop to murder by witchcraft? It seemed preposterous. And yet, it was true the woman hated her and that they were rivals for Scott's affection. Perhaps Olivia wasn't all that sure she'd won him?

As it turned out, Olivia and Scott ran into Tony and Fernand in the lower hall and followed them to Kathy's room, curious as to why the black man was there. Molly, her itching ears ever alert to what was going on the household, managed to trail behind them discreetly, as though she had business of her own to attend to upstairs.

184

Kathy turned an embarrassed shade of pink as the four came trooping into her room.

"What's going on?" Scott wanted to know, glancing from his excited son to Kathy and back again. "You seem nervous as a cat, Tony, and I'd like to know why."

"Aw, Dad . . ." Tony shuffled his feet. "Fernand thinks somebody may have planted a death *ouanga* in Kathy's room. He's gonna look for it. Say, Kathy, maybe it's good to have witnesses, huh?"

"Death *ouanga*!" Scott appeared incredulous. "What are you talking about? Who'd want to hurt Kathy? Fernand, why should you think such a thing?"

"This is ridiculous!" protested Olivia, and it seemed to Kathy there was a note of hysteria in her voice.

Molly was outside the doorway now with clean towels draped across her arm, as though this were the time to go about changing the ones in the bathroom.

"Me search, m'sieur?" Fernand addressed Scott. "Den, if I find, we talk."

The possibility that he might know something kept Scott from interfering as Fernand went over the room inch by inch. He searched the wardrobe, the drawers, even felt under the furniture and turned the rocker upsidedown to see if anything was taped to the underside.

He found nothing.

Finally, he had Scott help him lift the mattress off the double bed and set it on the floor.

"Look!" Tony pointed to the boxspring.

It lay there facing up. Fernand took it into his hand carefully and examined it, then held it up for all to see.

"A voodoo doll!" said Scott, aghast.

A heavy silence fell over the room. No one moved or spoke, frozen by the thing in the black man's hand. It was a small, white rag doll with features crudely drawn in red, and it was dressed in a lavender polyester garment. Stitched to its head was a clump of honey-gold hair.

"Kathy's hair! From what I cut?" The horrified

185

whisper came from Molly, who had moved into the room.

"The dress—it's made from one of my blouses," said Kathy in a small voice. The missing blouse. So she *had* brought it with her.

Fernand felt the head of the doll with a tentative finger. And glanced at Kathy. "You not feel pain in de head, mam'selle?"

"No!" She gulped. "Well, just a headache." Adding quickly, "I get them once in a while. It has nothing to do with that—that *thing*."

Slowly, Fernand drew out a long straight pin from the head of the voodoo doll.

"Scott, tell the man to take that ugly thing away and burn it," said Olivia.

"No! Must not burn," said Fernand. "Mam'selle's life burn up with it."

"To believe in any of this is blasphemy," protested Olivia. "Scott—"

"The point is," Scott interrupted, "who put that vicious thing in Kathy's bed?"

"Bet I know," muttered Tony, with a dark glance toward Olivia that no one could miss.

"How dare you!" she cried. "And what about that friend of yours? You gave him some of her hair, didn't you?"

"Think before you speak, Tony," his father cautioned. "That's a serious accusation."

"Need pointed scissors," said Fernand. Molly hastened to get them for him, ridding herself of the towels on the way. Meanwhile, the two men replaced the mattress on the bed.

When Molly returned, Fernand seated himself on the floor and began cutting the stitches that held the strands of hair to the effigy's head.

Kathy's headache was easing up. The aspirin, of course, she told herself.

With extreme care, Fernand snipped every stitch that held the crudely sewn body together, until the stuffing dropped out: cut-up bits of lavender cloth from Kathy's blouse. He felt through them and came up with some fingernail parings.

"Kathy was clipping her nails when I cut her hair," volunteered Molly.

"And *she* was in the room." Tony scowled at Olivia.

Scott glanced at Olivia, his eyebrows going up slightly.

Fernand gathered up the conglomerate that had represented Kathy, and stuffed everything into his breast pocket. "I take away, send to de wind." His eyes turned toward Olivia accusingly, and she moved back a step. "Dat woman, I saddle horse for her last Friday. Den I go to fetch water, but when I see where she head, I follow. To de bad *mambo* she go. Give her small package. For to make voodoo doll, maybe?" And with that, Fernand left the room.

"It's a lie!" Olivia's face had gone white. "Surely you don't believe him, any of you? Scott?"

A pulse was beating at Scott's temple. His gray eyes bore into hers like bits of steel. "You were present during the cutting of Kathy's hair and fingernails, Olivia?"

"So? I'm not the only one."

He nodded. "True. Both Molly and my son had access to those cuttings. And either of them could have taken Kathy's blouse from her closet. Except for one thing. They both love her. Can you say the same for yourself, Olivia?"

"Scott, really now—" she began, but he cut her off brusquely.

"Fernand did saddle a horse for you last Friday morning. I saw you ride off from my office window. Now he tells us you went to the *mambo*. Only someone bent on evil would visit that woman. And Fernand has nothing to gain by lying."

Guilt was written plainly on Olivia's face. For once her thespian abilities failed her, for the evidence against her was overwhelming.

Scott went on in a remote voice, "You did want me

to send Kathy away. I refused. And the next morning you rode into the forest. Need I say more?" The beautiful redhead seemed to shrink into herself as he stared at her grimly. "Strange. I feel as if I'm seeing you for the first time, Olivia. I suggest you go to your room and start packing. You're leaving here tomorrow."

Chapter Fifteen

Three weeks had gone by. Three weeks in which Kathy had taken pains to ensure Scott Blackburn was aware of her as a desirable woman and possible helpmate; and she did it by being sweet and feminine without artifice. By keeping her best foot forward. By holding back any sharp retorts when he irritated her, which was seldom now. By letting him know she admired and looked up to him.

Gone were her scruples about setting her cap for him. Since she loved him, why not? Had she but followed Molly's sage advice from the beginning, she wouldn't have had to go through that fiasco of emulating Olivia Borelli; she could have won his love before that temptress arrived. Never again would she permit pride to rule over love in her heart. Scott Blackburn was the only man in the world for her, and she was determined to become his wife. Though she might not be on a par with him socially and culturally, her love, she felt, could surmount anything. She was intelligent and quick; she would study so as to be able to share his interests. All along, Molly had insisted she was the right mate for him. Yes, she was right for him—because she truly loved him and wanted to make him happy.

And he was responding to her. Almost a thing of the past were the mercurial flareups, and she was careful not to add fuel to the fire when he did lose his temper. He seemed to enjoy her company both in the office and out, and many were the hours they spent together—riding, hiking, swimming. Tony was ever welcome, and his father could not help but note the closeness between him and Kathy. He could see she'd make a good mother for his son, she thought hopefully.

It wasn't long before she was convinced Scott loved her. She could see it in his eyes when he looked at her, hear it in his voice when he addressed her. Yet . . . he never mentioned love. He never kissed her.

She spoke to Molly about it, because Molly seemed to have an answer for everything. Molly was her mother away from home, and the wisest woman Kathy had ever known. Wisdom, she reflected, seemed not dependent upon an academic education. It was a special gift.

"Molly," she began, her forehead crinkled pensively, "Scott loves me, I'm sure he does, even though he hasn't put it into words."

" 'Tis nothing new to me, dearie."

"Then why doesn't he kiss me? Do you know he hasn't kissed me even once these last few weeks we've been spending so much time together? Yet he kissed me when I first came here. And I know he kissed Olivia."

"He didn't love you then. Nor Olivia," said Molly promptly.

"You mean, it's *because* he loves me that he doesn't kiss me? Molly! That doesn't make sense."

"Sure and it does, lass. He knows good and well that once he takes you in his arms he'll be breaking down and asking you to marry him, won't be able to help himself. I see you forgot the problem, eh?"

"Oh, I-I guess I did forget, what with everything so nice since that woman left here. Molly . . . what shall I do?"

"Can't say offhand, Kathy. It'll come to you, I'm sure. Everything else has been working out right, hasn't it?" Molly rolled her eyes heavenward. " 'Tain't nobody can tell me God don't answer prayers. I been bombarding Him for weeks. I should know."

For the next several days, Kathy pondered the question of Scott's mental block. He still needed to break through that subconscious drive to punish himself for Joan's untimely death. If only he would talk to her about it. Get it out in the open. Examine it realistically. Might he, once he declared his love for her? Was that the trigger he needed?

How could she get him to say "I love you"?

The solution came to her spontaneously one day while going down the stairs to join Molly and Tony in the kitchen for a game of Monopoly. Scott was at the bottom starting up, and it reminded her of the time he had saved her from a bad fall. Hadn't he ended up kissing her?

Should she or shouldn't she? There was an element of risk, but . . .

It was like replaying a familiar scene, as she gave a little scream and saw him leap to break her fall. For a moment he swayed with her in his arms; then, partly regaining his balance, he managed to twist so as to fall in a halfway sitting position, with Kathy sprawled on top of him.

She turned on his lap and sat up, gasping, a bit frightened yet.

Brown eyes looked deep into gray. His arms were still around her; they were close, so close. Surely, loving her, he could not push her away?

She felt as though her breath were suspended.

Oh, please, God.

Scott's arms quivered, then tightened about her. She could feel a tremor surge through his whole body, and she was trembling herself.

"Kathy?" he whispered. "Oh, Kathy, I do love you!"

A little sob escaped her. He had said it.

Tenderly, his lips brushed her eyes and nose and cheeks, nuzzled her ears, pressed deep into the soft hollows of her throat . . . then traveled upward to claim her mouth hungrily. She melted against him with all the fervor she had kept dammed up for so long.

When, finally, they drew apart, he said huskily, "I

want you to marry me, you know that. Will you, my darling?"

Would she! She stared at him out of big brown orbs, and the joy within her breast seemed almost more than she could contain.

"Oh, Scott," she breathed, "I thought you'd never . . . Oh, I love you so!"

He drew her to her feet. "Kathy, there's so much I want to share with you, so much I must tell you." He pressed her to his heart, his chin resting on her hair, and they stood quietly that way for a long sweet moment.

So much he must tell her. About Joan? Somehow Kathy knew that was what he meant.

"Well, now, did you ever see a prettier picture?" It was Molly, standing in the kitchen doorway with Tony by her side. Both were grinning like imps.

"You're gonna marry her—righto, Dad?"

"What do *you* think. Scram, you two, I want to kiss her again."

"Yes*sir!*" Tony made a victory *O* at Kathy with his thumb and forefinger—and when she did the same behind Scott's broad back, he snickered. Molly pulled him into the kitchen and closed the door firmly behind him.

Kathy snuggled against Scott with a happy sigh. "Is this a staircase romance?" she chided. "Oh, Scott, to think that Haiti brought us together. Who would have thought of finding romance in this strange land." She crinkled her pert nose at him. "Know what? I just might turn our love story into a novel. *Heartthrob in Haiti*—how's that for a title?"

"Corny," he said, tweaking her nose. "Now close your mouth and be quiet, like a good girl," he commanded.

"Yes, Mr. Blackburn," she said meekly.

And then there was no need for words. The way their hearts were throbbing said it all.